While Matthew and Jason investigate a series of murders in Washington, DC, Jacklyn and Nicolas start a long-awaited vacation with her parents.

Famous reporter David Callahan sets out with his girlfriend to have a good time and research the doings of a kidnapper prowling the woods of western Maine.

For all of them, the events turn out differently from their expectations.

Ruined Vacation
Copyright © 2021 Ann Raina
ISBN: 978-1-4874-3335-2
Cover art by Martine Jardin

Published by eXtasy Books Inc

Look for us online at:
www.eXtasybooks.com

Ruined Vacation
Nick and Jacklyn 7

By

Ann Raina

DEDICATION

Muse, you'll always be my best friend. You know too much.

CHAPTER ONE

Jacklyn invited Lesley to take a seat on the couch while she poured coffee laced with whiskey to warm up on a chilly April evening. Outside, rain drummed against the windowpanes while the wind was getting stronger. "And, my friend, how did you like being on Raiden's boat?"

Lesley blew over the hot coffee, smiling. "He'd kill you for calling the yacht a *boat*. Seriously, owners are very specific when it comes to the type of boat they're using. And—to put this right—I wasn't on the yacht during the ride. I met him at the Miami Harbor and greeted him with a bottle of champagne when he moored it."

"How nice." Jacklyn sat down and sipped coffee. She was still cold inside after a long day at her physiotherapy office where the heating system had failed during the last hour. "So, you did change your mind—at least a little bit."

"There's no harm in trying something new. To be honest—I wanted to do Raiden a favor. He was so thrilled to show me his latest creation. I couldn't stay at the pier and refuse his invitation, could I?"

"You're making progress." Jacklyn chuckled. After years of being a mistress and later owner of a dungeon, Lesley Gilbert had finally found a man to love, even without shackles to tie him down. "And . . ."

"Progress is a good choice of words." Lesley cocked her head, twitching her brows. She looked younger than her thirty-eight years, partly—Jacklyn was certain about it—because her lover was twenty-five. "You can't imagine what we

1

did in the bedroom. I admit he was . . . cautious, in the beginning. Too cautious for my taste. The first times I had to guide him, if you get my meaning."

"Small wonder. Usually, he could hardly wriggle his toes when you were with him."

Lesley laughed and bared her small white teeth. "Sometimes he was allowed to speak."

"Back then or now?"

Lesley snorted with laughter and had to put down her cup not to spill the contents. "Bad girl! I do allow him to speak, though I'm not fond of small talk while we're on it. He gets what I want—oh, was that a pun?"

"It depends on what's involved."

"Him and me. And a lot of laughter between the sheets." She stopped, still chuckling. "I sound like my old English teacher. Bad me! Boring! If I want him to, Raiden's a wild animal in bed, no shit." Lesley pointed a finger at Jacklyn. "Before you start worrying for me—though we both know he's well equipped—he's never rude. Really, never. I guess it'll take time for both of us to learn what's allowed and what's not." She made a face. "A little rudeness would really turn me on."

Jacklyn leaned back, pleased to listen to Lesley's story. She hadn't imagined that her best friend would find happiness with a much younger man, if with any man at all. Raiden had been her pet at the dungeon, and at first she had rejected the idea that a paying customer might want more than the treatment she granted him at the playrooms. Only when Raiden was abducted did Lesley admit her feelings and pray for his safe return. The FBI had freed Raiden in the end, but his affection for bondage games was lost.

"Do you hope that he'll return to your club one day?" Jacklyn asked softly.

"I'm convinced he'll want the games, not now, maybe not

in two months, but maybe in five. No man with his kind of sexual orientation will drop it for long. Yes, he's been through hell — he doesn't talk about it, but I heard from Nick about the cells and how other victims were abused. Don't get me wrong — it's not important for me, for us. He's a fantastic lover. I don't know why I didn't see that or why I denied myself the pleasure for so long. He told me that he fell in love with me instantly. Imagine that!" She growled. "Don't laugh, Jacky! That's not fair!"

"Oh, I'm not laughing." Jacklyn forced her laughter down to a chuckle, but seeing Lesley's mocking frown ruined her intention. "But it's so funny listening to you. He was there — for a year! He was right in front of you. A good-looking dude, as exotic as a man can be, and you knew more about the size of his ass than about the expression in his eyes, obviously."

"I'm serving the men's needs," Lesley replied with mock seriousness, crossing her hands on her knees and giving her voice a high pitch. "I'm not one to study their expectations, especially not concerning any relationship with their mistress." She made a face and let her voice return to normal. "Usually, I'm better when it comes to judging men's characters. I was wrong, all right. Yeah, it's all right. Make fun of me."

Jacklyn bent forward to touch Lesley's thigh. "I'm not mocking you. I'm happy for you. But, still, yes, I'll mock you for not seeing the love in his eyes sooner."

"Funny. By the way, you're planning a vacation with your sub, Nicky-boy, finally? I recommend Miami. It was marvelous."

Jacklyn rolled her eyes. "I wish. Let's say we compromised. I convinced Nick to spend a few days with my parents at a friend's summer residence in Popeville. In return, we'll fly to Portland three days earlier and spend some time alone."

"On the road? That sounds like fun. Just the two of you, a

cozy motel, and a lot of shackles."

"No. The staff will let us in."

"It's a house with staff? Your parents know wealthy people."

"My mom makes the connections, my father just smiles and is as diplomatic as a diplomat can be. That's why they always get the keys to any kind of mansion, residence, estate . . . you name it."

"Sounds great—three days with your lover and no one there to scold you for groans and moans."

"The hitch is—the mansion lies in the wilderness, kind of. Sure, the housekeeper takes care of it, and we won't miss a thing, but it's pretty isolated, if the pictures can be trusted. My parents are happy about that. It's rare that my dad goes on a vacation, anyway. But if things go south—"

"You both have nowhere to go. Is that to be expected?"

"Let's say my mom isn't excited about Nick and will never be. However, my mom and dad want to see me, and I told them they couldn't invite me without Nick by my side. That's okay for a weekend, as it was last year for the holidays. Because of Nick's gruesome working hours, I cherish the spare time with him even more, so that I won't go on a week's vacation without him. They accepted the deal."

"Begrudgingly."

"Yes, my mom. My dad is okay with any man if he isn't some ignorant jerk from the street. He needs someone to discuss world politics. Days without clever conversations are days he considers a waste of time."

Lesley pulled up her legs and reached for the coffee cup. "Which means, the only bad thing that can happen is that you have to spend some time outdoors to escape your mom's bickering." She shrugged. "Doesn't sound so bad to me."

"Did you finally manage to unwrap all the wedding gifts?" Nicolas asked as he took off his winter coat. "It took you two lovebirds long enough."

Jason Beckham, fellow FBI agent and best friend for years, looked up from his desk and made a face. "Thank you for asking. Yes, we did. And the book Lesley gave us hit us like a bomb."

"How so?" Nicolas switched on his computer and thanked Jason for the full coffee mug on his desk. "It wasn't something . . . indecent, I hope."

"Quite the opposite." Jason thrust his hands in the air. "It's a guide to Feng Shui. You know the slogans— *Slow Down the Energy Flow, Give Guests a Reason to Pause*. This stuff. Now Elaine's all for it, and our home's completely rearranged." He shook his head. "Hey, it's kind of Lesley to spare us something like *Leather Whips and How to Use Them*, but she made an impression on my wife. I can't tell whether I like or hate it." He sighed, exasperated. "Give her my gratitude anyway. I know it was a short notice invitation for Raiden and her."

"It was kind of you to invite them at all."

Jason's expression softened. "Both you and Raiden had gone through hell the weeks prior to my wedding. Elaine and I thought . . . well, I wanted to see a smile on your face, if it was only for a moment. Not to mention, the couple entertained the guests without trying. Lesley was charming and turned some heads, but Raiden was even better. I bet he danced with all the women, despite the sour expressions of their husbands. He's a specimen full of energy." He frowned. "How's he faring these days? You mentioned he was in psychological treatment."

"He still is. But he's getting better. He's young, he has stamina, and he's got the determination to battle his fears. He'll make it. The even better news is that his love for Lesley changed her profoundly. If you ask me, she's a different person, a better person. Because of her love, Raiden will overcome his trauma. That's the good news among the bad memories we'll carry."

"Talking about good news. You're going on a vacation with your lovely lady. What's the destination?"

"We'll take a flight to Portland — Maine, not Oregon — rent a car, and drive the rest of the way to a residence close to Popeville. It's in bumfuck country, and I'm stuck with her parents." He sighed. "The only bright spot is that we're going early. Three days just for us, travel time not included."

Jason smiled broadly. "Hey, you've bested serial killers and almost broke a kidnapper's every finger. You'll find ways to deal with Jacklyn's mom, right?"

CHAPTER TWO

David Callahan leaned back against the rough bark of the tree and stared at the fresh green leaves ruffled by the wind. "Spring in Maine," he mumbled as he wiped away tears. "Seemed such a good idea at the time."

Exuberant like any reporter hooked on a new story, he had invited his girlfriend Rebecca to join him on a trip to Portland and farther into the country, a kind of *road trip with extras*, as he had called it. Rebecca's expression had told him it had better be an exciting trip, or she would leave him for good. Their relationship had hit a rocky road during the last three months, and she was considering changing companies and leaving Bangor as well. Which meant she was willing to end their relationship and earn more money in one swoop. David knew he had one last chance to show her she was the woman he wanted at his side.

At the rental car office, he had complimented her on her new glasses, on her make-up, her haircut and color — this time a flaming red with a soft wave that suited her oval face — and he had, at the same time, surveyed the surroundings unobtrusively. To avoid complications, David had kept to himself that he wanted to solve the mystery of the seven missing couples and write a big — and for him life-changing — story about it. Rebecca would have cut off his head knowing that her investigative reporter boyfriend was misusing their vacation for inquiries. David knew her temper — if she found out about his intentions, she would leave him on the spot, even in the wilderness, and take the car home to Bangor without looking back.

"No good deed goes unpunished."

"Done packing?" Jacklyn asked, standing at the bedroom door.

Nicolas turned and stopped breathing. He would never get used to his lover showing up in yet another taunting sexy nothing that didn't deserve the word *clothing*, even in a generous interpretation. She wore a combination of dark red leather patches and many fine laces that covered the triangle of her pubic hair and parts of her bosom. A matching pair of high heels completed the incredible outfit and caused Nicolas to drop the pants on the suitcase.

"Well, yes." Coherent thoughts slipped away as well as his saliva. His mouth was dry and his expectation rose as to what she might be up to.

"Now you'd better shut your mouth before your jaw drops to your knees." She came to him as if presenting her shapely legs and womanly hips on a catwalk and gently closed his mouth with her fingertips. She kissed his lips sensuously, then pushed him on the bed. "Let's see what you've got under that awful mass of clothes."

With these words, she began to undress him, and he marveled at the love shining in her eyes and the slight wickedness that showed in her smile. He was blessed with a woman who was both a thrilling partner in bed and an intelligent executive. Over the period of five years, she had built up a physiotherapy practice that employed two fulltime physiotherapists and two assistants. She had a long list of patients with more coming in every month, mostly recommended by those she treated successfully.

"I don't think I should return the favor," Nicolas said as he ran a finger along one of the laces. "Or you might stand here naked."

"Oh, and that would be a shame." She kissed him and let her tongue fool around.

The motion stirred his arousal, and he returned the kiss feverishly, but stopped following her when she pulled away.

"Are you in the mood?" she asked softly.

Nicolas was not mistaken in having thought that the evening of their departure would develop into an hour of cuddling on the linens. Jacklyn was kind enough to ask for permission though her intention was clear. "Yes."

She kissed him again and allowed him to caress her close-to-naked body. "Very well, my Beast, let's have some fun."

As a kid, Keith Boswell had loved playing among the many washers in the big front room of the coin-operated laundromat in Livermore. His mother had chatted with neighbors while little Keith ran around or played with his toy planes, pretending that the tops of the washers were the airports. When they started rumbling, it was like an earthquake. The warm room smelled of washing powder, softener, and sometimes of bleach. The women spent their time exchanging the latest rumors while the laundry tumbled, and his mother knew everyone's story and added her two cents to the gossip. Maybe this was nothing special in a small town, but to Keith his mother was an example of a wise woman who knew everything that was worth knowing, much more than he read in his books. But she didn't just have talent with the customers. She had a knack with the machines and could repair every model, be it washer or dryer, so that it was operational the next morning.

She told him that every woman should know how to repair things, for there was no guarantee that a man would be around to take on the job. His mother had a distinctive look and tone of voice when she talked about men and Keith's father specifically. She made it clear to her only son that women should never rely on men, no matter the subject. After that statement she lamented time and again about Jeffrey's inability to take care of his wife, his son, and the business. She complained about Jeffrey running into the woods in a time of need, and that he hadn't stood his ground when the laundromat was robbed. The gangsters had ruined several machines and threatened the family before escaping with the cash. The police never caught the hoodlums.

Keith had been too young to recall the details of the assault, but he had memorized his mother's bleeding head wound and the picture of his father delivering the money with trembling hands, begging the armed goons to spare his family. When the gangsters grabbed the moneybag, they pulled Keith onto the street and let him go when they reached their escape van. Keith had sat on the sidewalk, crying his eyes out until his father came to tell him to go back inside. His mother had sat on the ground, holding the rifle in her hands and shouting at the top of her lungs *why the hell* Jeffrey hadn't shot the assholes when he had the chance.

With each repetition, the story sounded more like her father had just begged for his own life and not for that of his family. Keith looked at the bullet hole in the wall behind the cashier's desk as if his mom had left a reminder of his father's cowardice for everyone—but especially for her son—to see and remember.

He emptied the boxes at the washers, counted the money, and decided to take it to the bank to pay his bills. He reached for his baseball cap and his long-worn winter coat, put the sack with coins into a leather bag, and left the warm room for a cool and windy night.

"Now you won't go anywhere, my beast."

"I bet." Nicolas turned his hands in the shackles that tied him to their extraordinary bondage bed. Because he knew his mistress loved his struggle, he tore at the restraints and tensed his muscles, showing off with what he had.

She reacted instantly, parted her lips, and took shallow breaths while her fingers trailed his muscled chest and abs. She bent to kiss him but made a detour to bite his nipples gently. Nicolas moaned. He couldn't wait for her to tease him more while he was tied by his hands and feet, ready to be devoured. Jacklyn kissed his navel and let her tongue trail down the way to his half-erect member. He wanted to tell her to hurry—he couldn't remember ever being so horny—but he knew better. His mistress for more than three years had her rules when it came to treating her sub. She wouldn't tolerate any demands but instead withdraw and punish him for misbehavior—certainly with glee in her eyes. The game was as thrilling as it was frustrating. Nicolas held his tongue but lifted his hips. She saw through the move and cocked her head to look in his eyes.

"What did you do all day, my wonderful beast? Nothing but boring paperwork? You're much too eager for a man with a suspenseful job."

He grinned. "Suspense? Not like this. I was looking forward to this moment, ma Belle. And the view is outstanding."

She wiggled her butt. "You're flattering me while you're bound to the bed. I could leave you to watch my favorite show on TV."

The joy in her voice betrayed the threat. "You wouldn't leave me here, not with the view *you* have."

Jacklyn laughed merrily. "I was wondering—is your cock getting bigger?"

He lifted his hips. "I'm always striving to impress you."

"So you are trying to tell me something with that eager piece of manliness?"

"Since it's the only part I can use to catch your attention—yes."

Jacklyn almost collapsed laughing. "Then I'll grant your best piece all the attention it deserves."

Nicolas forgot about words when her tongue touched his glans, lingered for a second, and went down his shaft in slow motion. She repeated the move until his skin trembled and he shivered with suspense. He pressed his head into the pillow and closed his eyes. The thrilling ride toward the climax was better than the moment of highest arousal—he never knew what she had in mind and how long the ride would last. His heartbeat accelerated, and he clenched his fists.

Jacklyn tied a leather ball divider around his scrotum, glancing at Nicolas both lovingly and wickedly. He loved the sensation, the mix of pain and pleasure, and the assurance that he belonged to her. On these occasions, Nicolas regretted not having met Jacklyn sooner in his life. She was right for him in every way.

He gasped when she closed the last lace. By now, his erection told a clear story of how he wished the night to evolve, and Jacklyn massaged his perineum, touching his bound balls now and then before she returned her attention to his shaft.

"And now that everything is set for the ride, we're going places."

At the bank, Keith drew his baseball cap deep over his face and hoped to make the delivery without meeting anyone. He was mistaken. Albert Whannell, once a classmate, was a teller now and—to Keith's misfortune—always there like an old piece of chewing gum that stuck to the sole of his shoe.

"Hi buddy, how're you doing tonight?"

Keith despised the slimy, obviously mocking way of welcome. Back in school, Albert — *Big Al* to his mates — had used every free minute to taunt the much lankier and weaker Keith. Now Albert wore a fine gray suit that generously covered his paunch and pretended he was the friendly guy from the neighborhood. He claimed that the old days were long gone — *let bygones be bygones,* he used to say — and that they could be grownups and deal like gentlemen with each other. Keith knew better. He saw the glee in Albert's eyes that had always accompanied him when meeting with Keith, and he wished he hadn't made the detour to the bank.

"Hi, Albert." Keith poured the coins into the machine to have them counted and booked to his account.

"Business is good?"

"As usual." Keith prayed for the machine to count faster.

"I would like to introduce you to some new investments programs that we have exclusively for long-time account holders. Interested?"

"No." Even if he were interested, Keith wouldn't tolerate staying longer than absolutely necessary in the man's company. He sweated as much from the warmth inside the bank as from his building aggression.

"Come on, Cr... Keith, don't be so negative. Our programs are profitable. I could show you flowcharts of — "

"Not interested," Keith said decisively.

For a second, both were listening to the rumbling coins inside the counting machine.

"See, that's your problem, buddy," Albert went on with a deep frown. "You've always pushed away all the prosperous possibilities in your life. Look at me — I made it through high school, I graduated from college, and became a teller. Two years from now, I'll be bank manager and make even more money. You should take me as an example and turn your life around. It would be worth it."

The machine stopped, and Keith retrieved the account slip for the booking. "I own a shop. That's enough for me."

"It's a shop your parents ran, after a fashion. They barely made enough money to sustain your family—and you know that pretty well. I remember you wearing your clothes long after they didn't fit you anymore."

Keith breathed deeply. He remembered the mocking voices of the other kids when he came to school in too short pants and shirts that were anything but fashionable. It had been bad to be a slow learner. It had been worse to be the butt of jokes because of worn out and mended clothes.

Albert nodded gravely. "Your father went hunting, and if I have it right, your mom did that, too, just so that all of you had enough to eat." Albert lowered his wobbling chin and made a face. "And now you own that dreadful shop." He shrugged. "And you run it the same way. With less income every year."

Keith inhaled sharply when Albert wiggled his brows. "You—"

"Ah, don't make a big deal out of it. I know the numbers of every account. I'm a teller, you know. It's my business to know how much you've got in your account."

"It's private," Keith said defensively but knew that Albert wouldn't let go.

"Yeah, sure, private. It's your money, I know that. That's why I offered you an investment. Maybe you could earn some decent bucks in a few years, if you invested cleverly." Another shrug followed, and Albert's tone indicated he didn't take Keith to be clever. "Be as it may, Crab, crawl back into the sand, if you like. Just don't claim that it was my fault."

Keith pushed the slip into his jacket pocket, turned on his heels, and left the bank. He was so furious he bit down so hard that his jaws hurt. He was sweating badly now and stank even through the winter coat. As on many occasions before, he hadn't used the opportunity to smash Albert's face, to wipe that complacent grin out of his features, and ruin that asshole's nose while he was on it. He knew he had the strength to wrestle the fat guy and beat the living daylights out of him. His hands clenched to fists. While sweat trickled down this spine, Keith hurried back to his beat-up van, sat on the driver's seat, and pounded his forehead against the wheel until he felt better.

Nicolas strived toward the moment of release, the moment of no return when the arousal was painful due to its intensity. He kept his eyes closed and enjoyed the tight restraints around his wrists, knowing he could tear at them with as much strength as he liked without going anywhere. Venting his power without hurting his lover was one of the gifts of bondage. The other was a mistress who knew how far she could go to give her partner pleasure, pain, and orgasms that pushed him right into heaven.

Jacklyn lifted her body and broke their connection, but only for a second, just to let him know she could prolong his sweet torment if she wished. With an exclamation of purest joy, she let his shaft slip back inside her, so close to her climax she was shivering. Nicolas didn't make a move but allowed her to dictate the rhythm. As a reward, Jacklyn cried out blissfully. It was the sign for him to let go. One more thrust took him over the top, and he let his orgasm roll him under.

CHAPTER THREE

Back in the days, in his first job, David had already proven that he was willing to go further than other reporters. He was like a terrier — he bit into a story and didn't let go, no matter how hard he was shaken. His eagerness to uncover the truth had got him into trouble before, but a good reporter stirred unrest and made enemies. That was the way he pursued a story until he gathered all the facts and presented it to his publisher. Once the report was printed and collected merits, David smiled and relaxed until the next suspicious information hit his desk. He never let go when the circumstances were rough and his personal integrity threatened.

"Rough?" he said aloud. "This is a fucking grater, and it's rubbing my ass!" For the umpteenth time, David looked at the thick metal cuff around his left ankle. It was connected to a chain that his kidnapper had wound around the tree and locked with a large padlock. For the umpteenth time, he stood, grabbed the chain and leaned back until the chain was taut. He put all his weight into pulling the chain, hoping against hope that the weakest link would break and set him free, finally.

"So that was the first time I traveled first class. Quite a luxury for two hours."

Jacklyn linked arms with Nicolas on the way to their rental car. She was beaming with joy. "See it as a positive — my parents want to make this a special vacation for us. Look, the car's not average, either."

"Quite right." Nicolas admitted the sight of the large new SUV astounded him. The black vehicle with lots of chrome details had everything a driver's heart desired. He looked forward to the ride. "Yeah, fine, smile, my wonderful Belle. You got me." He stowed their luggage in the trunk that was big enough to sleep in without feeling constricted. "You could've taken all of your equipment and still have room."

"Charming. But we're here for a week, not a month." She slapped his butt. "Don't say I'm neglecting you. You'll get your share."

"Ouch." He bowed deeply to her like a humble servant. "But I'll be happy and forever grateful if we cuddle, of course." He held the door for her. "Or more."

Jacklyn settled on the seat and fastened the seat belt. She looked up and gently touched his cheek. "I'm happy to spend time with you without being interrupted by nightly phone calls and endless investigations that take you away from me."

He kissed her lips and prolonged the moment, bursting with happiness. Jacklyn looked so lovely, he wanted nothing else but hold and kiss her. "This week is just for us," he said softly. "I'll simply forget about your parents and spend my time just with you."

"Aww, that's so sweet my teeth hurt. Get in. It's a long ride, but the mansion's really worth it."

He slipped behind the wheel, as excited as any man about to drive a car worth a hundred thousand dollars. The engine came to life with a rich humming sound. "Let's go on a wonderful ride."

Keith Boswell liked airports. The thunder of the airplane engines and the hustle of hundreds of people on the concourse and the shopping areas reminded him of the stories his mom had told him when he was a kid. She had placed pictures in his mind while telling vivid stories of tough pilots and happy passengers, of charming crewmen and the many people who shared a flight to the same destination. His mom had claimed her father had been a pilot flying for one of the big companies, but Keith learned after her death that she had made this up. Her father had left the family when Shelley was eight years old, and she had never seen him again. When the police and the local priest offered help to locate him, Keith declined.

Nevertheless, Keith loved to spend time at the airports, either in Portland or in Augusta whenever he could afford it. He used to hang out for half a day, watching the passengers carry their luggage through the large concourse and other ones who called or whistled for a cab, impatient to ride to their final destination. People in comfortable clothes or in fancy outfits went through customs and directly to the rental car companies, exuberant about spending time in a foreign city while grumpy business travelers with expensive carry-ons snapped at drivers who had come to fetch them for a ride to town. Keith preferred watching the vacationers and listening to their conversations. Sometimes he was glad to be single. Sometimes he envied the happiness the couples shared. If he wanted to, he followed them, listened to their conversations, and tried to find out as much as he could about them. They didn't notice him or consider him suspicious. That never happened.

Keith bought a newspaper and pretended to read. When he turned around, he caught the fragment of a particular couple's joyful conversation. Spontaneously, he decided to follow them through the airport to their rental car, then watched them stow their luggage while they laughed and exchanged kisses and slaps on the butt. They appeared pleased as punch to spend the coming days together and joked about escaping into the wilderness like a hunter and his wife. She was a few years older than he, and Keith was intrigued about their relationship.

He memorized the license plate and turned to fetch his car, hoping that the couple needed time to adjust to the handling of the unknown vehicle so that he could tail them when they left for their destination.

"That's not the direct way to Popeville," Jacklyn said as she checked the navigation on the display. "You're making a detour? Why?"

"That's a question only a woman can ask." Nicolas grinned. "It's fun to drive. I don't need to speed. I don't need to be there at a certain time. Think of it—just the two of us in an amazing new car on a trip to remember."

She blew him a kiss. "All right. Proceed."

"Thank you." He drove for a while and enjoyed the handling and the rich sound of the three hundred horsepower engine under the hood. The road was rough, but the SUV handled every bump like a pro. "Do you know what I'd like to do? Replay our first real date. It was fantastic. You were so elegant, so powerful. You had your very own way of telling me what you wanted. It was amazing."

Jacklyn put a hand to her bosom and opened her eyes wide. "Seriously? You liked my dominance that evening?"

"Yes, I did. I was speechless."

"And that without being gagged. All right. That's . . ." Jacklyn chuckled. "Surprising. Honestly, I thought I pushed you pretty hard that night. I didn't leave you a choice."

"I didn't want one." He glanced at her. "You were the first woman who didn't expect me to read her mind and act on thoughts she didn't share. You told me what you wanted. It was my choice to either follow or not. And, yes, I wanted to follow you. You won me over that night."

"You wish to turn back time and live through that fantasy again? That can be arranged." She smiled. "Though there's no concert we could attend beforehand."

"We can listen to some classic music." Nicolas was warming up to the topic. "And you can ask me to enter your room to . . . seduce me."

Jacklyn laughed. "Oh, you scoundrel! You know that your participation is needed."

"I volunteer." Nicolas steered the SUV toward a deserted recreation area and stopped. "Sorry for the interruption, but I really need to see a man about a horse."

"I thought that only happens to women." Jacklyn twitched her brows. "Well, then, hurry, my Beast, I can't wait to get to Popeville, fancy car or not."

Keith's heart skipped a beat as he watched the SUV pull over. Excitement crawled through him like a drug, and he was addicted to it on the spot. Everything else was forgotten like it had been locked in a box. Heart beating in his throat, he bit his lower lip as he slowed down to stop ahead of the SUV, at recreation area exit. He knew he had little time—the couple wouldn't stop here for a picnic, just to follow a call of nature. He had two minutes to prepare what he needed and make his move. The need for speed fed his excitement in a mysterious way. He felt as if he had taken drugs and couldn't stop giggling when he got out of his car.

He told himself that if it didn't work, he had another chance at their destination. Couples like them—so he assumed—had plenty of time, enjoyed every minute together, and acted as if they didn't care for anything in the world. He bet they had rented a fancy cabin in the wilderness, but close to a town so that they wouldn't miss the amenities they were used to in their day-to-day lives.

They wouldn't see him coming. No one ever did.

He closed the door quietly and limped toward the SUV, groaning pitifully, and pressing one hand on his thigh. He waved to gain attention. "Help me, please."

The woman in the passenger seat looked up, made a face, and left the car. She closed the door and came closer, not bothering to button her winter coat.

"Can I help you, mister?"

"Yes. I . . . I stumbled and fell and now my leg's on fire." Keith reached her and stood with a deep sigh. He tried to smile amiably. "I'm so glad you're here. I don't think that I can drive any longer."

The woman reacted to his smile sympathetically. She had brown wavy hair and a fair complexion—not a beauty, but a good-looking woman in her thirties. She pushed a strand of hair behind her ear.

"Do you want me to have a look? I'm a physiotherapist."

Keith hesitated. She looked like a rich woman and spoke without distinguishable accent, and yet she was helpful without prejudice. In his lifetime, he had suffered rejection so often, he knew her friendliness had to be an act. No one ever considered him worthy of any help. He hid his distrust as best as he could.

"Yeah, that would be kind."

When she made another step in his direction, he pulled the small stun gun out of his coat pocket and rammed it against her midsection. She stared at him in disbelief, went into spasms, and collapsed without a shout. He caught her unconscious body, stowed the gun, and carried the woman to the cargo area of his van in less than two minutes after stopping on the shoulder. Sweating profusely, he turned around to face his second opponent.

The woman's husband exited the woods, wiping his mouth

and putting away a handkerchief. He looked around and exhaled, grimacing as if in pain. From the distance, he looked positively ill but was quickly aware of the van parking ahead. He was alarmed when he didn't find his wife on the SUV's passenger seat.

"Jacky?" He turned around and when he didn't see her, rounded the hood of the car. "Jacky, where are you? Don't play pranks on me!" His glance fell on the parked vehicle again, and without hesitation or doubt, he reached inside his long jacket.

Keith stood up behind the open passenger's door of his van and used the upper rim to rest the barrel for a controlled shot. He aimed carefully. The man wore a winter coat and a thick pullover.

His mother had taught him to stay vigilant. Focus. Aim. Shoot. Don't get distracted. You must see everything and react in an instant. If you look away or miss anything, your prey escapes. Though she had spoken about deer, the rule applied.

At no other time had this rule been more important. Keith noticed that the blond guy was reaching for a gun. Without losing a second to wonder and fear, he pulled the trigger and hit the man's neck right above the collar. The guy was fast, much faster than Keith anticipated. His hand shot up to pull out the anesthetic arrow, but it was too late. The dizziness set in immediately. He put both hands on the hood to steady himself, but within seconds, his knees buckled. He tried to reach for the gun again, right before he collapsed beside the tire and lost consciousness.

Keith gave up his stance and stowed the rifle on the passenger side. Releasing the breath he had been holding, he tied the woman's hands with a zip tie and glanced at the road now and then. There was no traffic in sight, so he backed up the van to manage the hardest task—pulling the heavy man into the cargo bay. Keith sweated and cursed as he thought about the best grip to lift him across the low rim. Though Keith was stronger than his slender frame suggested, the man weighed more than a hundred and eighty pounds, and the dead weight of an unconscious body was even harder to maneuver.

Sweating profusely and at the end of his rope, Keith pushed him inside the van, closed the doors, retrieved the fallen arrow, and went to take a drink. Only when he felt better did he tie the man's hands, frisk him thoroughly, and pulled the *Glock22* out of its holster. He weighed the weapon in his hand, then stowed it at the small of his back.

"This was a close call," he whispered, relieved that he had shot the man with a rifle at long ranch. He got weak knees thinking of a confrontation with an armed husband. It was a nightmare to think about that dude pulling his sidearm to confront Keith on the road.

The next inner pocket contained a badge, and Keith's breath quickened again. He had caught a federal agent and his wife. "This will be an interesting afternoon."

"Eureka!" Matthew leaned back with a satisfied grin and rubbed his hands.

Jason looked up from his keyboard. Typos were his constant companions, and he was grumpy because his fingers seemed to hit all the wrong keys. "What's the sudden joy?"

"I found the missing link."

"The missing link in what case?" Jason hit the backspace key and deleted the last sentence. Somehow, he couldn't find the right words to describe the FBI proceedings at the latest crime scene. Sullivan, boss and monster in total union, would rip his head off and chew on his eyeballs if he didn't deliver a text that was easy to read and contained all details. Jason remembered the last time Senior Agent Sullivan had browbeaten a seasoned agent for his insufficient summary of events. Even though the agent had his head left in place, Jason decided to avoid that mistake. He wanted to keep his eyeballs, too. "We've got a bunch of cases on the table."

"*The Mutilator* as some agent called him. Four women dead. Mutilated faces. Do you remember that one?"

"Oh, the one that only hit our desk because the last murder was in Fredericksburg and one of us made a query, right? I could throttle him for that."

"Correct. I found out the serial killer's motivation. Where are you with your thoughts, Jason?"

"Sullivan dropped five cases on our desks with the scathing remark that he has more in store and that we'd better hurry. So how should I know which one you picked? Why did you look into this one?" Jason rubbed the bridge of his nose. Though it was only noon, he was tired, grumpy, and longed to go home to his wife. She was eight months pregnant, and he tried to spend as much time with her as possible. He couldn't help but sound petulant. "All right. What's the big breakthrough?"

"Do you remember the first widower's statement to the FBI — after the bureau took over the case — that he recognized the first names of two victims? He told the agents that his wife had been with five other girls in a clique at high school."

"So?"

Matthew pointed at the many sheets of paper he had spread on his desk. "The agents in charge didn't investigate further but handed the case straight to us. That's why I just read all the statements of the widowers and friends of the victims, and then I found out that a young woman named Margie Winters, maiden name Margie Ellwood, once belonged to that clique but no longer after a car accident. She was eighteen back then."

Jason frowned. "What do you know about her?"

"She spent eight weeks in the hospital because of several

injuries. One of them left her face partially paralyzed. The injuries were treated with professional care, but no doc could help with damaged nerves."

"You got the hospital file?"

"No, the file room suffered a flooding last year, but I got my hands on a short summary of the case where the injuries were cited." He pointed at the sheet of paper. "Margie continued her life, married, and had a son. She died eighteen months ago — suicide. Her husband had died in a work accident ten days prior, and — I speculate here — she saw no reason to live on. There was no letter to her son . . . or so the son claimed." He shrugged. "Since it was an obvious suicide, the police closed the case."

"A month later, the murders began." Jason sat up straight, his typo-riddled report forgotten. "And all victims had their faces mutilated prior to the murders."

"I think that Margie's son Terry knows something about what happened after the car accident." He held up the DMV photo. "Maybe she told him the truth behind it or something else that might be useful."

In an instant, Jason stood, grabbed his jacket, and left the desk. "Let's find him and hear the story."

Though Keith's mom had taught him good manners, he had no need for them. At school, the children had either made fun of him or overlooked him like an old toy in the corner. Once, the teacher forgot that he was a participant on a trip with the class. The bus returned after ten minutes to fetch him. His teacher was heartbroken. Being overlooked was also useful. The same year, Keith observed his teacher having a liaison with the principal and blackmailed her to grade his geography test though he hadn't rightfully passed. At other times, Keith vanished and no one missed him. He wreaked havoc in the chemistry lab at school during an English lesson. When asked, he claimed he had been in his class, and no one was able to prove him wrong.

As a grownup, he could sit in a diner and watch people because most of them turned their attention elsewhere after a brief eye contact. Keith's face wasn't attractive. When he looked in the mirror, he heard the sentence in his head that he had a face *only a mother could love*. He wasn't tragically ugly, but he had a crooked mouth and narrow eyes, and as if God had had a bad day creating him, he had thrown in skin rash that made his face look like a landscape with different shades of red. When agitated, his face reddened in unhealthy patches.

Right now, he looked like a map of pink and purple spots, and his lower lip was bleeding because he constantly bit it. He was alone behind the wheel, and his victims weren't stirring, so his looks were irrelevant. The husband would be out cold for about two hours, and if the wife moved, she couldn't escape. The doors were locked.

Keith was content he could do what needed to be done.

Matthew fastened his seat belt. "Amber Fowler was the first victim. She lived in Cumberland, but she was born and raised in Westbrook, close to Portland."

"In Maine, yes." Jason filtered into traffic while Matthew fed Terry's address into the navigation system.

"The same goes for the second victim, Shelley Morgan. She attended the same high school and moved away after graduation. She was murdered in Portland." Matthew grinned. "That applies to the third and fourth victim, Madelaine Green and Samantha Eldridge. The last one was murdered in Fredericksburg, and Agent Burke researched and found out about three similar murders. Which indicates we're dealing with a serial killer. The women knew each other."

Jason frowned. "A lot of girls knew each other at that time, and there were many groups that they belonged to, certainly. Why did we get this damn case?"

"You're in a bad mood today, huh? Because Agent Burke and his partner were dealing with eight other cases at that time, and anyway Fredericksburg is in our district. Don't be glum. This could be interesting. Back to the case. We know from photographs that Amber and Shelley were with them. Margie left while the others graduated together and stayed in contact, more or less."

"You think the other women wanted to hush up what really happened or who was responsible?"

"We only know that Margie—obviously—never got back in contact with her old friends anymore."

Margie Winters's son Terry was not at home. Neighbors told Jason and Matthew they had seen him leave the day before in the morning, and he hadn't returned yet. His old *Ford Escort* was gone, too. The neighbors claimed that the old car couldn't be missed because of its noise. They also reported that Terry was often gone for a day or two, sometimes longer over the weekend. He lived alone, and no neighbor had witnessed visitors during the last weeks. Upon further questions, the neighbors assumed the young man used the apartment only to stow his belongings and lived elsewhere. Everyone said he was a friendly man, always helpful, and with good manners. Matthew called his employer, and the kindergarten principal told him that Terry would begin his work in the early afternoon.

Jason sent an attempt to locate Terry Winters to all police stations hoping that his car would be spotted on the streets.

"Who's the last woman on the list?" he asked when Matthew stubbed his cigarette.

"Carla Demasio. She left Portland for DC to work here. If the information can be trusted, she's single, has no kids, lives alone, and her only relative is a sister in Maryland. If Terry is involved—"

"Let's find Carla and take her into custody."

"All right." Matthew sat down on the passenger seat and looked up to Jason. "You coming?"

Jason rounded the hood and slipped behind the wheel. Every time he worked with Matthew, he felt outmaneuvered, as if he'd missed important parts of Matthew's speech or action. He couldn't help considering the older agent like a sophisticated classmate, who was always one step ahead and knew things Jason didn't consider. In his imagination, Matthew had a list in which he noted all of Jason's obscure behaviors and rated them at the end of the day. Not for the first time, Jason was angry that Matthew had found the missing link in a case. He expected that Matthew would mock him throughout the day.

His mind was still working on the half-finished report he had left behind when he drove through Arlington toward Carla Demasio's home. Her employer had told Matthew on the phone that Carla had taken a week off for vacation, and he didn't know whether she had left town.

Matthew found out Mrs. Demasio's cell phone number, but she didn't pick up.

"Maybe she forgot it," Jason said.

"Or it's low on battery. Or she's in the bathroom and doesn't hear it ring." Matthew went through the file on his lap. "I wish we had found that missing link sooner, but no one listened to Mr. Fowler. At that time, Amber was the first and only victim, brutally murdered but just one of the many cases of the local homicide division." He looked up. "If I have it right, the homicide division was dealing with a case of missing tourists."

"Missing? Why was that a homicide division case?"

"Because none of the missing persons ever showed up."

"How many people are we talking about?"

"I don't know. Since there is a pattern behind it, the FBI field office in Portland is on it."

Jason glanced at him, brows raised. "I'd better not ask. They might request us to help. That won't be easy."

"I wouldn't want it easy," Matthew said with a deep frown. "If I had wanted an easy job, I'd have become a teller or something similar like a clerk or a company manager."

"I can't imagine you sitting behind a desk and studying numbers on a screen."

"Yeah, probably not."

"What do your parents do for a living?"

"My mom doesn't work, and my dad repaired airplane engines. He had the hang of every kind of machine. They talked to him — so he claimed. And you?"

"My father built up a small company producing auto motor parts."

"*Beckham Select* is your dad's company?" Matthew asked, incredulously staring at him. "They don't just make motor parts, they're the leading company in manufacturing tuning parts."

"Yes, that, too." Jason wished he hadn't mentioned his father. He didn't like the open admiration for what his old man had accomplished, starting with nothing but a good idea.

"And you allow Nick to drive most of the time? That's surprising. You could have the finest cars if you wished."

"I decided to stay independent." Jason parked the car in front of a garden with hundreds of flowers planted in artful arrangements. The graveled path led to a one-story building with a small porch and a swing. One of the windows was open, and the wind tore at the white curtain, giving the impression of someone lurking behind it.

Jason noticed that the front door was open a crack. Without hesitation, he pulled his sidearm and approached the porch with measured steps. He heard Matthew behind him. Jason stopped and listened in front of the door. The silence seemed like a bad omen. After a brief eye contact, Matthew stepped forward and pushed the door wide open.

"FBI! Anyone home? Mrs. Demasio?"

Aside from the doorknob slamming against a cupboard, the house was of an eerie silence.

"Mrs. Demasio?"

Matthew moved forward carefully, looking left and right. Jason followed close behind, expecting anything from a drowsy house occupant to a criminal with a pointed weapon. He took a left turn at the corridor when Matthew took a right. The rooms were sparsely furnished in a classic white, with red pillows on the couches and chairs. There were no knickknacks on the shelves and cupboards. Mrs. Demasio either loved a Spartan lifestyle or didn't use the apartment regularly. Jason stopped when a large black cat crossed his path, in flight of something or someone he didn't see. It vanished through the open front door.

Heart beating in his throat, he entered the woman's bedroom. The linens were tousled, the pillow had dropped on the carpet, and several pieces of her clothing lay scattered on the chairs and the floor. The door to the adjacent bathroom was open and the light above the mirror was still on.

Upon a closer look, Jason found dark brown soil on the carpet in the shape of the sole of a shoe. Considering the cleanliness of the house, he assumed that Mrs. Demasio wouldn't walk into her bedroom wearing dirty shoes in a man's size.

"Matt! Over here!"

Matthew appeared on the doorstep. "The house is empty, the front door was opened with a skeleton key. What did you find?"

"Someone was here, and I bet he didn't come for a chat." He pointed to the stains on the carpet.

In the bathroom, Mrs. Demasio's toothbrush lay in the sink, and a cup with water stood on the rim. The room smelled of a rose-scented shower gel. The towel beneath the cabinet was wet, and her nightgown lay on the floor.

"The room is still warm and wet. She can't have been gone for long."

"Gone?" Matthew holstered his sidearm. His look and tone of voice were grim. "This looks like a crime scene to me. She was abducted right after taking a shower." He smirked. "The kidnapper took her away clean as a whistle." Before Jason could scold him for his weird humor, Matthew turned away to call the CSU team and issue a missing person report for Mrs. Demasio.

Jason rested his hands on his hips and exhaled slowly. If this case didn't solve itself, he wouldn't be home with his wife before nightfall.

CHAPTER FOUR

K eith clenched his teeth. His euphoria about the sudden and wonderfully unexpected coup had made him forget about his empty fridge. He remembered too late that his plan for the day had included grocery shopping in one of the large centers in Portland. Temptation had overwhelmed him, and he'd forgotten his plan. He heard his mother talk inside his head. She scolded him for not thinking about groceries earlier in the week.

He locked the house door again and went back to his van, regretting deeply that he hadn't stolen the wonderful new black SUV. He knew he couldn't afford to drive such a luxury car that would be traced quickly via GPS signal—he had heard Albert talk about it one day—but nevertheless it would have been fun to sit behind the wheel, even if it was for just once in his life. He had never possessed something of value and longed for a time when he would be rich. A credit card with an unlimited amount of money—that would be fine. A new van with many extra features, a new heating system for the cabin. With that, so he hoped, he would be able to keep a woman happy and make her love him dearly. Everything would be easier once he had money and a car. He had a wish list at his door, reminding him every day of the things he wanted to possess.

"First the work," he recited one of his mother's phrases.

Grumpily and with his stomach reminding him of the empty fridge and shelves, he opened the back door. Mrs. Hayes looked at him with wide eyes full of fear, while Mr.

Hayes, FBI agent and incapable of taking care of his wife —
just like Keith's father — opened his eyes drowsily. Keith
clenched his teeth to regain control over his overbearing hatred. In his mind, he used a bat or a piece of pipe to batter the
husband in front of his wife. While she cried for his life, she
would understand that her fate would be the same and that
no one was there to help her — certainly not her husband.
They were both lost because they were unfit for life outside
their warm home. He could tell by their appearance that they
spent an easy life with lots of amenities. It galled him that so
many people had it so damn easy they didn't cherish what
they had.

"What do you want from us?" Mr. Hayes asked. His speech
slurred, and he took in deep breaths when he moved.

Keith pulled the agent's gun. "Get out! Now!"

The wife looked at her husband pleadingly. She wanted to
talk to him, but then only whimpered. He lifted his tethered
hands in her direction and looked her in the eyes. She pressed
her lips together and nodded briefly.

Keith's anger rose with every passing second. In his mind,
he repeated that he had a plan he would follow, but it was a
close call, even closer when Mr. Hayes didn't move immediately but grimaced as if he were in pain. Keith had expected
that the effects of the anesthetic would wear off without aches
of any kind.

"You either get out or I'll shoot you right there!" He com-
pensated for his high voice by aiming at the woman. "You can
bet that no one will ever find you."

He got the expected reaction.

Mr. Hayes lifted his shackled hands and tried to climb out
of the cargo area. "Don't hurt us. We'll do what you want."

Keith couldn't tell whether this was a prepared speech
agents learned in Quantico, or if the agent was trying to gain
time and show cooperation while checking out his escape

route. No matter the reason, Keith loathed that the husband spoke as if Keith were a brick short of a load. He would show him his cleverness and not grant him time to think of a way out. "Walk and walk fast. Don't think I'll hesitate to shoot you."

"I understand." The agent stood on wobbly legs and bent at the rear fender for a moment as if to catch his breath. If this wasn't an act, the drug had affected him harder than Keith had anticipated.

He made a step back, farther out of reach so he wouldn't be fooled. In the noon light, the man appeared tall as a tree and at least half as wide. If he hadn't been fully concentrated on the task ahead, Keith would have applauded himself for the accomplishment of putting the hunk into his van in the first place. The time in the woods had made him stronger, and he felt a surge of pride.

"Over there!" He watched the couple as they slowly, step by step, made their way across the yard. The agent looked left and right, apparently memorizing the surroundings, while his wife kept contact to his left arm and appeared shocked to the core. She wouldn't make a wrong move.

More than a year ago, Keith had prepared a chamber in the earth. At first, it had been an occupation to calm his raging mind after the brutal death of his mother. When it was done, he'd covered it with a metal grating and a locking bolt. While he'd built, he'd heard his mother's voice in his head as she'd explained the tasks he was bound to fulfill. He'd been eager to listen, and he'd listened well. The chamber's walls were smooth without a chance to find a hold. The grating was strong and heavy, the locking bolt mounted on an iron plate, screwed to the construction.

Keith pointed at the long ladder he had put into the chamber. "Down there, and make it quick!"

"Into the hole?" Mrs. Hayes asked with terror in her voice.

"Please, no!" She made a step back. "Don't do that to us. Please! Don't let us die here!"

He loved her despair. "Go down there. Now!" A slight drizzle set in, and Keith smiled. "You'll find your abode very comfortable."

"What do you want from us?" the agent asked as he made eye contact.

Keith sensed his horror, but it wasn't for his sake, just for that of his wife. For a second, Keith hesitated, then said, "Climb down that damn ladder!"

"But—what for? What will you do with us? We are just a couple on vacation. We mean you no harm."

"Shut up! Don't try anything or tell me I shouldn't do it. Get down there or die on the spot." He pointed the gun at Mrs. Hayes' head. "Do you want to watch her die?"

Mr. Hayes turned to his wife. Keith loathed their look of love and her curt nod of compliance with the inevitable. He wanted her to cry and break down while he tried to soothe her. He wanted her to understand that her husband couldn't give her solace. "Hurry!"

Mr. Hayes took hold of the rim and made his way down carefully, now that the steps were wet. Mrs. Hayes bit her lip-stick-red lips while tears trickled down her cheeks. She sobbed as she wiped them away.

Keith liked that. She wouldn't try to attack him. He had her cowed, and her gaze confirmed that she believed he would kill her without a second thought. Keith's agitation lost its momentum. He would get what he wanted—a little later than planned, but still to his satisfaction.

His stomach grumbled. He wanted the moment to be over so that he could finally leave. He longed for ham and eggs, and the smell of fresh brewed coffee. He decided to drive to Livermore even though he wouldn't get his preferred brands. His hunger grew by the minute, as if he hadn't had a decent meal for weeks. He didn't like going hungry for a longer period of time. His mom had claimed he had a fast metabolism and needed more food than other people. There were times when this condition appeared in unpleasant intervals.

"Now you!" he barked and waved the gun about while he stayed far away from the chamber's rim so that he wouldn't fall even if she dared to launch an attack.

She avoided his stare and shuffled toward the rim. She reached for a hold with trembling hands.

"Careful," her husband warned her and lifted his hands to catch her should she fall. "You can make it."

Keith grinned. When she reached the bottom, he stowed the sidearm in the small of his back and pulled out the ladder quickly, allowing the couple no time for countermeasures.

Mr. Hayes put his tethered hands around her. "I'm so sorry, Jacky, that I wasn't there for you."

Keith scoffed loudly. "You can't protect her. You left her alone, ran away when she needed you. You just thought of yourself! I'll show her that you aren't worthy of her. You shouldn't raise children." He spat out. "That was your mistake."

Mrs. Hayes cried harder now as she stood at the bottom and couldn't get out again. With a thud, Keith closed the grating and pushed the locking bolt into its place. He stood for a moment and looked at their frightened faces. He enjoyed their fear as well as the fact that he was master of the situation. For a minute, he stared at the husband's regular features. He was a handsome man, someone who could get any woman he wanted. He had chosen an older woman, still pretty, and maybe richer than he was. In his mind, Mr. Hayes whispered sweet nothings to her, and she smiled about his flattery. Those days were over.

Grinning, Keith straightened. The picture of the couple locked up for good and waiting anxiously for his return would accompany him throughout the ride.

Like in the old movies, he walked away whistling a tune.

Panting heavily, David sat on the wet soil again. Like many times before, the thick chain had mocked his meager strength and remained intact. He couldn't break the chain, and he had no tools to pick either lock. He wasn't the strongest man, just a guy who did sit-ups and could bench-press a hundred and fifty pounds. He didn't spend much time in a fitness gym when there were stories waiting to be told.

"Trapped for good. That bastard knew what he was doing." David ran a hand through his hair. It was a gesture he had trained to perfection — mostly used to gain a woman's attention. That was why he wore his hair a little longer at the top — more for the women to play with. Some called him the *Master of the Flirting Game*. He was handsome, had muscles in the right places, and he knew how to move. He could dance, too, and impress the women with intelligent monologues about the latest frauds, scandals, and corrupt politicians as well as their methods to increase their power. If he wanted to, he could twist any woman around his finger.

His boss had told him that the secret behind good newspaper reports was not just excellent research, but the ability to loosen the witnesses' tongues. Most people don't like reporters. All journalists were considered intrusive and unreliable to tell the truth. If you wanted information, you had to be charming and persuasive, even compelling. Good looks, good manners, and outstanding preparation led to stories that were both true and convincing. David Callahan was a serious reporter, and the best-selling newspaper in Bangor paid him a great salary for his outstanding abilities in journalism.

Right now, David would have given all of his famous stories and prizes to have the key to the padlock and be able to run away.

Nicolas held Jacklyn tightly in his embrace while she sobbed. He murmured soothing words while he thought about their situation and how the goon had tricked them. He didn't doubt that the man had done this before. He was bold, experienced, and knew the surroundings. The technique of shooting a man with an arrow to knock him out took time to learn. Usually, such excellent shooters worked for the army or had served before, but this hoodlum was in his mid-twenties and therefore too young to have such experience. Whatever their kidnapper did for a living, he handled his rifle like a pro. Nicolas mused about the arrows—this man wasn't a killer for fun. He wanted his victims out cold but kept them alive for something that would happen later. Staring along the smooth chamber wall, he wondered whether the villain would leave them in this place to watch them die slowly or take them elsewhere. A shiver ran down his spine. His next thought was that the bottom of the chamber was much too clean to have served another couple as a place to die. That wasn't much solace but sufficed for now.

Jacklyn looked up to him, sniffling. "What took you so long in the woods? I thought you just wanted to relieve yourself."

Nicolas pushed away the image of their slow death. "I don't know what I ate or drank, but suddenly, my breakfast wanted to see the sunlight again."

"Ow."

"How did he get you?"

"He pretended he was hurt, and I offered help."

"My advice to—"

"I'm helping people. That's what I do. Yes, I threw caution in the wind, left the car, and he overwhelmed me with some kind of stunner."

"Did he—"

"He had no time, I bet, to do anything else than drag me into his van."

Nicolas exhaled. "Small mercies that I'm grateful for. Did you see where we were going?"

"No. The van didn't have windows."

"Do you remember anything about the roads he used? Did he drive on a highway?"

"No, the van wasn't going fast, and some of the roads were full of potholes. I also heard gravel banging against the car."

"That means he avoided big roads with more traffic." He nodded as if that would solve the riddle of their abduction. "Did he stop for gas?"

"No." Jacklyn lifted her chin so he could kiss her. "You know I'm afraid that something might happen to you every day when you leave the house. I'd never thought that I'd be a part of that danger. I mean, I'm a physiotherapist! I lead a simple life. I wanted to take some days off from work with you, and now we're in deep shit. We sit in a hole six feet under—"

"Don't say that, Jacky, please, it's got a bad ring to it."

"Okay." She slipped from under his arms and searched for a handkerchief to blow her nose.

He made eye contact. "We're not dead yet, and we aren't buried alive. Whatever this goon wants, he needs us to be alive to do it. We have to fulfill a task—something his crazy mind came up with. He wants to put us—*me*—to a test. He'll—"

"—put me in a precarious situation and make you try to save me. Yeah, that's what I thought."

"I will save you, Jacky, right away." He lifted his chin to look at the grating. "I don't know what's on his mind, but we won't wait to find out. He's gone for now," he concluded when the van took off, spilling gravel.

"Is that FBI profiler talk or my lover who wants to soothe

me and restore hope?"

"There is still hope. We can get out of here. Here—I kicked some stones into the cell when we walked here. One of them must be sharp enough to—wait. I've got something even better."

Jacklyn bent to find a sharp stone. "Better than this?"

"Yes. Do you remember that I told you the inner pocket of my jacket is torn?"

"The usual." She straightened with the stone in her hand.

He was relieved that she was concentrating on the task and not on the misery they were in. The less she thought about the crazy goon's intentions the better.

"You stuff your coins and other things into them and wonder why they tear apart."

"Right, but my Swiss Army knife slipped through. It's in the bottom hem. He didn't find it."

"You carry a knife in your long jacket?"

"Don't you?" he asked with a smile.

"Women carry purses. And mine is still in the SUV." She groped for the knife. "Do you think the police have found our car by now?"

Nicolas hated to burst the bubble of hope. "We took a detour, didn't encounter much traffic, and stopped somewhere along the road. No one is searching for us. No one knows where we are, or how far he drove with us." He frowned. "For how long was I out cold?"

"Two hours, give or take."

"That was a heavy dosage."

"You scared me, Nick."

"I'm sorry."

"We're on our own." She ripped the lining and retrieved the knife. With a smile that should convey strength but was obscured by worry, she showed him the small blade. "But not lost."

He lifted his hands so she could cut the plastic. "No, my love, we aren't lost." He kissed her chastely. "And we won't get lost." He freed her, too, and opened another tool in the knife set. "Here we go."

"A screwdriver. What do you want to do with it?"

"I can't do it. But when I put you on my shoulders, you can reach the screws."

"And why not push the bolt?"

"It's in the center of the iron plate. You can't reach that far. That's why you have to unscrew the plate and pull it together with the bolt."

"You just made this up, right?" Jacklyn shook her head, obviously amused in spite of their situation. "You can't know that."

"I looked at the construction when we stopped at the rim. It's rather simple — but effective if you can't reach up."

"I bet he didn't think of that when he overwhelmed us." She crouched to open her shoelaces and take off the shoes. "What did he do with you that you were out for so long? I was really worried."

"He shot me with an arrow. He's an excellent marksman." Nicolas bent to lift Jacklyn onto his shoulders. "If this doesn't work, you have to stand on my shoulders, okay?"

She looked up to the grating. "I don't see this happening, Nick. Who knows how long these screws have been exposed to the weather?"

"We don't have another choice. If we can't get away before he returns—"

"All right. Don't frighten me. I'm frightened for both of us."

Nicolas chuckled as he put his hands against the wall to have a more stable stand. "Can you reach the screws?"

"No." Jacklyn let the screwdriver slip into her coat pocket to have her hands free. "Remind me that I need to do more workouts. I don't know—" She sighed. "Did I mention that I'm scared of heights? That I'd never climb anywhere higher than a ladder?"

With his support, she knelt on his shoulders. It was a precarious position, but the only one from which she could reach around the iron plate and not hit her head at the grating.

"Catch me if I fall."

"A music quote in the wilderness. I'm impressed."

"I'm scared shitless," she replied breathlessly.

"You're gonna make it, *ma chérie*. I know that."

"How can you be so sure? Oh, wait." She balanced her weight by inching forward. "Think positive, huh? Never believe in a bad outcome."

He understood and moved closer to the wall so that she could put her knees against the hard soil. He stabilized her even though he almost hit the wall with his nose. "Exactly. Take it like an adventure."

"*Fantasy Island*? I hated that show." She reached up and put the screwdriver to work. "I never understood why people find it fascinating to run through the wilderness."

Nicolas tried to breathe evenly though she held tight with her thighs to his head. "For some it's a dream come true."

"A dream? My dreams are very different from this here." She whined. "It doesn't move. What shall I do?"

"You have to hold the nut on the lower side. Pull your sleeve over your fingers so you don't scrape your skin."

She looked down. "Did you do this before?"

"I'm an FBI agent." He tried for a light tone, and she nodded gravely.

"It's in the manual for escapes in the wilderness."

"Some knowledge comes in handy."

Jacklyn followed his suggestion, but still whined that the screw didn't move.

"Try one of the others," Nicolas said.

"Okay." Jacklyn moved to the left and put the screwdriver into the screw slit.

Nicolas looked up. She was working hard, but it was a combination of skill and strength needed to loosen the screws.

"Try to scrape the sand away around the screw. Maybe that will help."

"It's sure a damn fucking trap. Fuck!"

Nicolas heard the knife hit the ground.

"I need to come down again." Jacklyn sounded close to tears.

"Do it slowly." He reached up her legs and helped her climb down along his body. "See? Done something you haven't done before."

"You're still trying to cheer me up? Brave lover." Jacklyn wiped her nose and looked at her reddened fingers. "The screws are tight, and I don't know whether I can move even one of them."

"Take a break. Your hands are trembling."

"What about your shoulders?"

"You're light as a feather."

"I've gained weight since we met."

"Oh, those were the days." Nicolas caressed her face, trying to convey confidence with every fiber. He didn't want to imagine what the criminal would do with them once he returned. "If I could lend you my strength, I'd do it."

"I know. I'm not so sure—optimism is a fine thing, but right now, I don't see us running away."

The CSU technicians turned Mrs. Demasio's house upside down to find clues to her whereabouts or to the stranger who had her in his clutches. The soil contained plant fibers, and Dr. Miller was confident he could identify their names and maybe their origins once he had the samples in his lab.

Matthew's investigation unveiled that Carla Demasio had only a few friends and none of them had seen her in the past few days. They described her as a reclusive person who wasn't out to make friends and lived her life alone most of the time, claiming she enjoyed her own company. She liked her job as an assistant to an editor with a widely known publisher, reading books, and doing power yoga five times a week in a women's gym and at home. Since she had moved from Portland, Maine, to the suburbs of Washington, DC, she hadn't changed jobs or her home, and wasn't a woman to go to parties or participate in events her company hosted. Matthew concluded that she had no boyfriend, who might have surprised her by showing up in her bathroom.

"I think she might be an old maid," he said when Jason returned to the living room.

"The kidnapper wears size thirteen shoes. We know that Mrs. Demasio is five feet two tall and corpulent. Would Terry Winters be strong enough to carry her away?"

"If he carried her. If he had a gun, she'd probably go with him without making a fuss."

"To his car and into it? There are no wet footprints outside the bathroom." Jason skipped through his notes. "A neighbor who walked his dog witnessed a gray van without any logos park in front of her house, but he didn't watch anyone go in or out because he finished his morning routine shortly after. Other neighbors were already on their way to work."

"Busy beavers around here. Any retirees we can talk to?"

"An old man across the street spends a lot of time at the window, but since the van parked with its end toward the house, he didn't see whether the worker put in anything more than his tools. He admitted that he had to leave his position several times for walks to the bathroom. He also couldn't remember the license plate or if it had one."

"Where are the gawkers when you need them?"

"It's a cul-de-sac. You don't have as many people walking the streets, and there are no traffic cameras, either."

"And the kidnapper knew this. Damn." Matthew looked around the room as if the evidence would jump at him once he looked into the right direction. He wished it would be easy. Just for once.

Jason called headquarters to find traffic camera footage from surrounding streets shortly after the possible kidnapping and told the team that the kidnapper had a thirty-minute head start.

Matthew inspected the small house once more, giving a monologue as he did so. "The kidnapper knows about her environment, has watched her before. He knows when she'll be at home and uses the minutes she's under the shower to break into her home and overwhelm her. He must have been here during the last few days, even weeks. He knew she had time off from work. Maybe he even talked to someone at the publisher. I'll check that." He flipped his cell phone open.

"We'll follow the trace of the van and ask if and when it was stolen." Jason shrugged. "If he had no plates, it might well be his van."

"I hope that the hostage rescue team has more luck." Matthew rolled his eyes. "In the meantime, we must hope that no one reports a mutilated woman found in a dumpster."

Back on Nicolas's shoulders, Jacklyn scraped the dirt away around the screw and tried once more to loosen it. She cursed and whined, but her efforts were rewarded when the first one turned. She removed it with a triumphant grunt.

"Only three more," she mumbled. Sighing, she went back to work.

Nicolas remained quiet. In spite of his stamina, balancing Jacklyn on his shoulders took its toll. She was of average weight, but the continuous pressure on his muscles was harder to endure with every passing minute. He hung his head and took deep breaths while the rain shower ebbed away.

"I need to come down again," Jacklyn said by a while. "There are still two left, but—" She sighed deeply, and he knew how she felt.

He helped her stand, but her knees were weak, and they sat on the ground.

"Take a break. It's all right." He kissed her with deep affection, becoming aware that he was more in love with her than a year ago. "I love your strength," he whispered and wiped away her tears. "You can do this. Just two more screws—"

"Or we're screwed? Yes, we are." She nodded emphatically and fumbled for her handkerchief. "If I can't turn those screws, this crazy shithead will return with a weapon and force us to—"

"Shh." Nicolas pressed his lips on hers again and held her when she wept. "Take your time. Recover. I bet he can't be back soon. We're a long way from the main road."

"Wherever we are." Jacklyn sniffled. Her gaze went up to the dark gray sky. "You think he's done this before, right?"

"Yes."

"It's the hideout of a serial killer."

"We don't know that. Don't make assumptions."

She bit her lower lip. "FBI work rules?"

He nodded once. "Stick to the facts, don't assume anything. Put together what you've got and come up with the correct conclusions. Jason uses a whiteboard to collect his notes and hints. It's a kind of mind map for everyone to see. We found out many connections just by comparing the details we had."

Jacklyn kissed his nose. "I love you more every day. You're the guy I want at my side—you're trying to make a story out of this gruesome situation. That's a gift." She sighed and got back on her feet. "Let's see whether I can work a miracle and get us out before midnight."

"Because at midnight the wolves come out?" Nicolas helped her settle on his shoulders once more.

"Because if we can't get out before nightfall, we're not only screwed, we're fucked up."

Matthew finished the call and shook his head when Jason looked at him questioningly.

"Nothing. If she was kidnapped, the kidnapper didn't contact her boss or any of her friends. She's got no relatives in DC, and her sister hasn't heard from her in months."

"Ransom is not the goal." Jason kicked the rear tire of their service car. "Damn it. We were just thirty minutes late." He looked back to the victim's home. "Let's find Terry, and quick."

Keith remembered his mother following a deer trail with the passion of a bloodhound. She never tired, never gave up. Seeing the prey, she sat motionless for long minutes and waited for the best moment to shoot. When she shot the prey and it dropped to the ground, she was excited — exuberant. More often than not, she bragged about her abilities and claimed rightfully that she shot much better than her husband did. After those tirades, his father went out on a hunt of his own, and if Keith had to accompany him, his father lamented about his miserable wife all day. If Keith didn't agree with him, his father's argument got louder, and he drank his cheap whiskey with the passion of a man who believed that alcohol would turn the world around and make his problems go away.

When the old man was already drunk, he called his son a *milksop* and a *weeping boy who would never grow up* even though

Keith was a teenager at that time. His father accused him of siding with Shelley every time and loathed his son's attempts at talking sense to him. Then the beating started, and more often than not Keith had no other choice than to run off into the wilderness to escape the fists and the bickering. On several occasions, he was gone for days, and he only came out when his mother appeared at his favorite hideouts. At age sixteen, Keith was a master of the woods, could survive for days without supplies, could shoot an animal for meat and build a shelter to stay dry. Though he wasn't the cleverest boy at school, he had survival instincts, was an apt handyman, and taught himself what he needed to know. His mother supported his independence and never scolded him for parting with his father without leaving a note. In fact, she appeared to respect his intelligence not to hang around with the loser of the family.

Keith always returned home. Though his parents quarreled every day and his home was a conglomeration of cheap furniture other people had thrown away, he had no other place to go to and was intelligent enough to understand that he needed education he couldn't find in the woods. At that time, he started to cut trees to build a cabin far off the main roads. He dreamed about leaving the town behind once he finished school. His intensions were fueled by his father's browbeating that led to real beatings more than once. Keith decided it would be wise to put as much distance between his father and him as possible.

While Keith walked through the small shopping center to buy groceries and supplies, his thoughts returned to the couple he had locked up. From the moment he had spotted them at the airport to the minute he had forced them into the hole, Keith's excitement had grown. Now he had a boner he concealed with his coat. For the first time, he had caught a couple with an older woman and the husband a police officer. It would be a challenge, he knew, to find their limits. He mulled over the necessary procedure while he put ham, bread, butter, and sausages into his cart. He went on to find his favorite brand of coffee.

Smiling, he paid cash and whistled while he pushed the cart to his van.

To Nicolas's astonishment, the last screw was the easiest. Jacklyn dropped it with a triumphant "Tada!" and stood on Nicolas's shoulders so that she could push back the plate with the latch. It was a challenge to her strength and balance to lift the heavy lid. Jacklyn cried out when she slipped the first time and the weight crashed down again. For a second, she swayed, and Nicolas feared she'd lose hold and fall down.

"Shit!" She panted loudly. "Any good idea how to push it open?"

"I can try and shove you." He held tight to her calves. In any other situation, this would be the clue to a sexy remark — something about her long legs and her underwear. Nicolas swallowed hard when he thought of the predicament they were still in. He had the bad feeling that their time was running out. "Ready?"

"Yes." She put her hands around the grating. "Do it."

Nicolas got down on his knees a bit and then pushed her up with momentum. Jacklyn thrust the lid with all strength so that it crashed to the other side.

"I did it!" she shouted.

"Yes, you did." Nicolas's heart hammered against his ribs, and he thought his shoulder muscles were torn. He clenched his teeth in pain. His legs trembled with strain, but he stood upright until Jacklyn reached the rim and climbed out. Only then did he put his hands on his knees to catch his breath and roll his shoulders.

"Run and get the ladder!" he urged. Standing alone in the deep hole, Nicolas feared that their kidnapper would return and catch Jacklyn. He wouldn't be of any help to her. Worse — he would stand in a hole in the ground, hear her scream and become witness of her suffering without a chance to change her fate. Until she returned, he prayed under his breath for another ten minutes alone in the woods. He was sick with worry that the one minute they needed would not be granted.

Jacklyn was out of breath when she pushed the heavy ladder into the opening. Nicolas tossed up her boots and climbed the steps as fast as he could.

"Let's go," Jacklyn said after putting her boots back on. "Let's run."

"No." Nicolas pulled out the ladder and took it back to where it belonged. When he returned, he took her in his arms. "As I told you — we're saved. Though you did the hard work."

Jacklyn patted his shoulders. "I know why I chose a tall man."

Nicolas closed the lid, put the plate and hatch back in place, and took Jacklyn toward the cabin. He looked at the lock and the metal bars that made a break-in impossible. "I don't believe this."

"What?"

Nicolas looked through the window after rattling the door. "The house is secured like one in Harlem."

She stood beside him and peered through the grated window. "You're right. Even the windows are locked."

"Either he's hiding a treasure in there, or he's more than just the normal sociopath." On the back wall stood a large cage, but he couldn't see whether there was an animal inside. He admitted that he didn't want to know.

"That's not reassuring." Jacklyn shivered in the cool air. "What are we gonna do?"

He looked around and decided to have a look at the shed

built close to the cabin. "We need some water, food, a phone." He tried the lock, but it didn't budge. Nicolas knew that if they were on flight without any supplies, they wouldn't last for long. "He's nuts about security. In the woods. This guy's a psycho for sure." He looked around. There was one path leading through the woods, most probably toward a major street. Tire prints told of its usage. "We have to leave."

"And not along the road, if I interpret your look correctly."

"We don't want to run straight into his arms, right?"

"Not again." Jacklyn pulled up the collar of her coat. "Okay, so we run away from the cabin and the street. Do you have any idea where we are?"

"Not really. We aren't far up — it's not colder than in Portland. However, if he drove for two hours, we're far away from Portland, and from Popeville as well. I bet." He made eye contact. "Would the staff call the police if we didn't show up?"

"Maybe in the evening. We're announced to arrive today. I didn't mention a time."

He took her in his arms and wished he could make her worry go away. Considering the small adventures they had mastered so far, this was their utmost challenge. He needed her to believe that they would make it by nightfall. "Hey, we're still alive, we're out of the hole, and we can run away. We'll make it."

Jacklyn held tight to him. "Please, Nick, get us out of here, fast. I'm scared shitless."

He knew that feeling.

Chapter Five

Police officers located Terry Winters in a craft store in Alexandria, and reported that he took his time choosing what he wanted to buy. The officers stayed in the parking lots in front and at the rear of the shop and waited for Matthew and Jason to take over the operation. They had also secured his car but not opened it, as the leading officer pointed out.

"Rick Morris," the officer said, shaking hands. He had the voice and bearing of a man of action, straight to the point and unrelenting. "We could storm the building in three minutes." He shrugged, pursing his lips. "Even if he's armed, we would take him down much faster than he could act. In and out—quick as a whip."

"If you're wrong, he'll take the customers hostage." Matthew kneaded his injured right hand while he squinted at the entrance. "You've got the building surrounded. He won't escape. I'm going in to talk with him."

"It's your call," Morris said, shrugging and walking away with his thumbs in his belt.

Matthew sensed the man's arrogance and that he would have stormed the building already and been done with the suspect. He was glad that the word of an FBI agent was still enough to keep eager uniforms at bay.

"He kidnaps a woman and then goes shopping—four hours later?" Matthew frowned. "If he has pulled this off, he has no feelings at all."

"Never underestimate the shrewdness of a criminal. What do we know about him? That he works as a kindergarten teacher. And that his boss appears to like him." Jason scoffed. "It would be the perfect disguise."

"Do we pretend to be customers?" Matthew asked Jason, who surveyed the parking lot.

"Yes, sure."

"You can stay outside if you—"

"Don't finish that sentence, or you're gonna need a medic to stitch your bleeding face."

"Ouch."

Jason strutted toward the door and ripped the door open forcefully as if he expected a quarrel. Matthew didn't dare recommend he should put on another expression, or the suspect would know of his profession quicker than anyone could call *FBI*.

Matthew hurried to follow his partner, reciting the protocol for a covert approach but knowing this wouldn't go by the book. Looking along the aisles, he applauded his decision to keep the police forces out. There were five more customers selecting items in various sections, and Terry Winters was one of them, carrying a basket filled to the rim with craft accessories, apparently for children. He was a tall, well-muscled yet slender man in his late twenties, wearing a casual blue dress shirt and new jeans. His fashionable haircut and his clean-shaven face indicated that he took care of himself. He wore a golden watch and a woven wristband around his right wrist. An older man with full but graying hair stood a step away from him. They were lost in conversation, chuckling now and then about an item Winters had found.

An elderly woman stood five feet behind them in the same aisle, murmuring to herself as she compared price tags on two packages of origami paper.

Terry Winters looked up, and no matter how good Jason's attempt was at looking like a harmless man from the street who had just decided to pay the store a visit, Terry appeared to know instantly who he was. He dropped the basket, said something to the man at his side, and then ran toward the rear door. The woman was pushed against the shelf so fast that she stumbled and fell. Terry was faster than Matthew at the end of the aisle. On the run, he hit a rack that spilled its contents on the gray floor. Matthew jumped across hundreds of small glasses filled with acrylic lacquer, stumbled, caught himself, and ran on.

"Jason! He's coming your way!"

Matthew rounded the corner, slipped on the floor, and skidded like a bad ice skater against the shelf at the rear wall. He gained speed again, pushed two more customers out of the way and saw Jason arrive from the left while Terry was already heading for the rear exit.

"FBI! Stop and turn around!"

The suspect glanced across his shoulder, eyes wide and full of fear. He rammed into a tower of boxes filled with spring decorations, and while the boxes scattered to the floor he changed course to head for the storage. Matthew overtook Jason on the chase, was a step behind Terry when he entered the large room, and tackled him forcefully. Both men went down. Terry grunted as he hit the concrete floor with his hands and chin, and Matthew knelt on his back, groping for his pair of handcuffs.

"Terry Winters, you're under arrest for kidnapping Carla Demasio."

The handcuffs locked, and Matthew turned the suspect on his back to frisk him. He took the wallet and his cell phone for inspection.

Terry squirmed on the floor as he tried to sit up. His chin was bleeding, and he grimaced with pain. "Kidnapping? Are you nuts? I was shopping here!"

"Shopping? Then why did you run?"

"This morning, you kidnapped Carla Demasio," Jason stated, out of breath and panting so loudly, Terry's answer wasn't understandable. "Where did you take her?"

"I kidnapped no one!" Terry shouted as Matthew helped him stand. Blood was dripping from his chin. "I was with a friend this morning!" He looked from Matthew to Jason. His face reddened, and his fear seemed real. "And why's the FBI here? I wanted to buy stuff for the kids at the kindergarten. They're expecting me to show them how to fold Origami birds today."

"The birds will have to wait." Matthew shoved him through the store toward the FBI limousine. "Tell me why you ran."

"Let go of me!" Terry couldn't hide that he was alarmed by the number of uniforms in the parking lot. "What's this all about?"

"You don't wanna talk? Fine with me." Matthew grunted. "Get in. We're taking a ride."

"No!" Panting, Terry broke Matthew's grip and made a step away from the open door. A strand of his dark blond hair fell over his forehead. "I didn't kidnap anyone! I don't know why you think that I've got anything to do with it!"

"Then why did you run?"

"Tell us where you keep Mrs. Carla Demasio." Jason stepped closer. "Right now!"

"Who are you talking about? I don't know anyone by that name!"

"Don't play dumb. She was kidnapped this morning, and you were unaccounted for the last several hours and not at home. We have reason to believe that you have something to do with her disappearance."

Terry opened his mouth and closed it again as if he found no words to express his excuse. He looked across the parking lot, then nodded once. "There are people in this city who have a life, okay? I don't need to leave a note when I spend my night elsewhere. I was with a friend. We talked. It was late. I stayed at his apartment. Anything else?"

"We asked at the kindergarten you're working. The chief didn't know of any girlfriend."

Terry took a deep breath, and his anger mellowed until he said, "I said I stayed with a friend."

"A good friend?" Jason asked. "Someone who'll give you an alibi for this morning?"

"Sure." Terry grimaced when he saw his own blood trickling on his shirt and pants. "Let's say he's a friend with benefits, and I don't want my boss to know. Do I make myself clear?"

Jason pushed him against the car forcefully. Officer Morris and his colleagues took note of the scene and made a move, ready to lend a hand. Matthew signaled them to stay away.

"It's clear when we say that it's clear. So far, you haven't said anything that exonerates you in any way."

"Take your hands off me!" Terry sidestepped Jason's fierce grip.

Matthew cleared his throat. Jason understood and let go.

"You're in a gay relationship. Fine." Matthew pulled out his notebook. "We need the name and address of your partner."

Terry's eyes narrowed as he stared at Jason, who didn't conceal his disgust. "If the principal learns about this, I'm finished working at the kindergarten." He turned his attention to Matthew. "Don't tell me about equal rights and that stuff. I don't want any trouble, but I want to keep my job."

"If your friend confirms that you were with him this morning, it's a start."

Haltingly, Terry revealed the name and address of his friend, but asked twice to have the man's name not revealed to his boss. He turned half way to show them the handcuffs. "Am I free to go now?"

"No." Jason stared at Terry, and his voice was down to a

menacing growl. "As long as your whereabouts aren't veri-
fied, you're the main suspect."

Terry huffed. "At least, take off the handcuffs. Please.
They're cutting into my wrists."

"Not until you tell us why you tried to escape."

Terry hung his head. He spoke slowly, as if he weighed
every word. "I have a weakness — sometimes I try to smuggle
some small stuff out of a store . . . without paying."

"You're a shoplifter?" Jason sounded disgusted. "You
want to teach children right from wrong but you steal from a
store?" He shook his head. "Man, I don't see you keeping
your job."

"Have you ever been arrested for shoplifting?" Matthew
asked, and wished he could send Jason to fetch coffee if only
to get him away from the suspect.

"When I was a youngster," Terry admitted quietly, staring
at Jason. His eyes were wide, and sweat trickled down his
temples. "Listen, whenever I took something, I made up for
it. I just can't . . ." He exhaled, grimacing as if revealing the
truth caused him physical pain. "Please, don't tell the principal. I wasn't shoplifting here. You can check all my pockets, if
you wish. I was choosing stuff for the kids, and I planned to
pay for it. That's the truth."

"But you ran." Jason raised his brows and put his hands on
his hips. "That doesn't look like something an innocent man
would do."

Jason's jacket was open, and Terry's glance fell on the
weapon. He swallowed and his Adam's apple jumped.

Jason continued staring at him. "Explain that to me."

"I panicked. Okay, I didn't mean to, but I panicked."

"You made a quite a show out of that, and you were close
to getting away." Jason shook his head. "I don't believe a
word. Get in the car. We'll talk about that at the office."

Under protest, Terry Winters sat down in the service car,

and Jason slammed the door. Matthew held him back when Jason wanted to turn to Officer Morris.

"I don't know what's eating you, but we're after a serial killer, not a small shoplifter."

"Did he already convince you that he's got nothing to do with it?" Jason scoffed. "Fine. I don't believe a word of what the guy said. I want to talk to this friend with benefits, and I want to ask the store manager whether Terry stole anything here, ever. Only then might I consider that his story has a pinch of truth in it."

Matthew let go of Jason's arm, frowning. "Is it possible you don't like gays?"

Jason stared at him, eyes narrow. His lips were a thin, bloodless line.

Matthew was speechless. Jason turned around to speak with Officer Morris, and Matthew lit a cigarette to calm his nerves.

The sunrays warmed David's body, and he was grateful for the bright weather. It helped to keep despair at bay. Though he might be able to collect rainwater, he might still die of hunger or exposure — whatever came first. The hunger pains grew stronger, and he rolled into a fetal position on the ground, enduring what he couldn't change and hoping for the cramps to pass quickly.

In order to digress from the misery, he thought about the story he had researched.

The kidnapped couples had more in common than renting an expensive car at the Portland airport. David had written the first serious article for the *Bangor Gazette*, titled *Where are they?* showing the headshots of five missing couples at the time. They shared three facts. They were between thirty and forty years old and looked better than the average. They weren't the beautiful models you see on catwalks, but also no normal people with crooked faces or bad teeth. All of them originated from the upper middle class, who could afford a nice vacation. If statements of the relatives could be trusted, their relationships were happy and they enjoyed time together. For three couples it was their first vacation in years. The other two couples had been touring Maine for the first time.

The FBI in Portland was on the case, so far without luck. Though the rental cars could be located via GPS in a fifty-mile radius around the airport, the persons remained missing despite intensive searches of the surrounding woods with dogs and helicopters. The FBI assumed the victims had been taken to a desolate area, killed, and buried shortly after. The reasons of the *MCK — the Maine Couple Killer* — remained a mystery, and the profiler statement consisted of assumptions that they were searching for a white male in his thirties who might have a handicap of some kind. He must know the woods intimately and was shy — a hermit more than a participant in regular town activities. It was presumed that he hated rich people or envied their wealth. That led to the further conclusion that the man lived in poverty, probably in a cabin in the woods. However, there were thousands of cabins in Maine's woodlands, and the police as well as the FBI had searched thoroughly without tangible results.

While David was developing the plan of a trip with extras, two more couples disappeared within ten days. Four more persons were lost in the woods and never seen again. David sensed the biggest story of his life and the ultimate chance to tell Rebecca that he loved her and wished her to stay with him.

He didn't intend to promise her that he would marry her — he wasn't convinced it would work — but he loved her in a way that justified going a great length to salvage their relationship.

He remembered Rebecca's frightened face and the horror in her eyes when the kidnapper dragged her away.

David covered his face with his hands and sobbed.

Nicolas turned away from the cabin, deeply regretting that they couldn't take anything useful with them. Without water and food, they wouldn't make it far. Not to mention that the night would be cool, though not freezing. Since he hadn't been interested in the trip in the first place, he hadn't prepared for hiking through the woods. All he wanted to do was spend time with his loved one—inside a heated bedroom.

He turned around when she slipped on the still wet soil and caught her hand in time so she didn't sit on her butt. "Are you all right?"

Jacklyn flashed a smile. "Sure, yes. And before you ask—I won't change my mind. I always wanted to go hiking in spring. It's beautiful here. So stop asking me and march on." As if to prove her good mood, she overtook him and walked with a swing in her steps that almost betrayed her fear.

"I don't intend to pamper you," Nicolas said quietly. With two long strides, he was at her side again. "It's a gruesome situation, I know, but when we keep going in one direction, we'll come to a road sooner than later." He pointed to the west. "We'll walk in a semi-circle so that we don't cross the path toward the cabin, but find the road, nevertheless. It's a question of hours."

"You're still consoling me and taking care of me." She glanced at him, and this time her smile was honest. "I'm convinced we can make it. If we don't fall into a crevice, crash down a bear trap, or drown in a river." She shrugged. "In any of these cases, I'll blame it on you, of course, and choose some-one else to be at my side. You know I have a bad temper."

Nicolas couldn't help himself. He stopped, took her in his arms, and kissed her. He needed to feel her warmth — that she was alive, still at his side, and breathing. When caught inside the criminal's van, he had lived through the ultimate fear of losing her. He had seen the muzzle directed at Jacklyn and couldn't tell whether the goon would pull the trigger or not. While he felt like shit, he hated himself for his weakness and that he hadn't reacted any faster at the SUV. He might've taken out the kidnapper if he had reached for his sidearm right away.

"I love you so much," he whispered. "I —"

"You won't lose me, my brave lover." Jacklyn caressed his stubbly cheeks. "If you say we can find the road, then we'll find the road. I hope this happens before nightfall, though," she said as they parted and walked on. "Because I haven't brought my nightgown with me. And I'm missing my beauty soap."

"Your soap, yeah." Nicolas's mind ran amok with the weird situation and that he knew nothing about the woods and what they would encounter. Meeting a raccoon or a deer would be fine, but a bear or a bobcat? "What about me?"

"You have a beauty soap, too? I should know this. You're my sub, and it's my task to take care of you. If you speed things up, we'll spend the night in a cozy hotel room, and I'll make you forget about soap and everything else."

Nicolas nodded with a small smile. The woods around them seemed to mock their pretended jolliness, and the leaves whispered ominous words he didn't understand.

"Terry Winters alibi turns out to be true," Matthew stated when he met with Jason at their desk. "Mr. Harold Foster, forty-seven years old, distinguished CEO of a building management, confirmed that he's in a relationship with Terry and that he was with him at the time in question. On their way, they passed several traffic cams, and that adds to his alibi. I sent him home." He put down his notepad. "You look like you ate something sour. Did you want Terry debunked as a liar?"

"Since when do you believe in statements made by the girl-friend . . . boyfriend? He would lie for him, of course."

"Terry Winters doesn't appear the type of guy who'd brutally murder four women. Look at the facts," he interrupted Jason's heated reply. "The killer researched the whereabouts of each of his victims, which means he needed a lot of spare time to go where he wanted. Terry Winters is a kindergarten teacher in a committed relationship. His partner sees him almost every day, and he has a job that requires his presence. We learned from the principal that he hasn't been on a vacation, and he doesn't have a job that requires leaving town." Matthew shook his head. "Despite your ignorance, he's not the guy we're looking for."

Jason grunted something unintelligible, emptied his coffee cup, and reached for his jacket. "If you're so convinced, fine. But think of it—the moment he identified me as a police officer—I don't know how he did that—he dropped everything and ran, risked hurting people on the way and destroyed merchandise. Does that look to you like the action of someone who was a shoplifter once but didn't intend on stealing something today? Well, if the answer is *yes*, you should rethink your attitude toward the suspect." He shook his head. "I'm going home to see my wife."

"You do that. Say hello to Elaine for me." Matthew watched him leave. He had a gut feeling that Jason would take a hot shower at home and cuddle with Elaine until he forgot about the suspect who was different from his expectation.

Matthew fetched a fresh cup of coffee and checked his emails. So far, the hostage rescue team had not heard from the kidnapper, and the team leader was pessimistic that he would make contact.

Pitying the poor woman, Matthew sat down to write his report about the latest developments.

CHAPTER SIX

On his way home, Keith was worried about the motor sounds. The van was seventeen years old but ran smoothly, usually, but still he accelerated carefully, aware that the engine cut out sometimes. Then the motor ran idle until the gas pedal worked again. The ride home took much longer than anticipated, and he decided to have a look at the engine right away. He had a shed full of spare parts and was good at repairs.

When the van coasted to a stop in front of the cabin, he remembered something else he needed to take care of. He pulled the key and got out, a half-eaten bagel in his left hand. Frowning, he rounded the hood, fetched the two paper bags with goodies for the next days, and looked at the locked grating ten yards away. His memory appeared to have the same cutouts as the engine. Chewing on the rest of the bagel, he was under the impression that he had finished a task before he went shopping, but he could not remember what it had been.

He unlocked the door and stowed the groceries in the fridge and on the shelves, gazing through the window now and then. Like a kid close to Christmas, he approached the hole in the ground and found the plate loose and the screws gone. His careful construction was destroyed. Blinking with surprise, Keith tried to put meaning to this strange event. Cocking his head and frowning deeply like his old man had done when searching for a coherent thought in his alcohol-riddled brain, Keith walked around the earth chamber, looked at the ladder at the shed, and back toward the grating.

Only then did the images of the man and the woman appear in his mind's eye.

He expelled his breath and ran both hands through his unruly hair. "Hayes. *Hayes*. Yes!" Keith stood with his mouth wide open and stared at the empty hole. "Gone. They're gone. How is this possible?"

Like an avalanche, the name of the couple set his memory free. He even recalled their frightened faces and that he had been determined to remember them. He couldn't explain the sudden gap and why he had returned without knowing about the couple anymore.

Now they were gone. Gone! Like they had wings and could lift themselves to heaven.

He had work to do. He had a rifle to load and ammunition to grab.

Panting heavily, Keith ran for the cabin.

Matthew wrote the report, checked for typos, and hesitated before sending it to Senior Agent Sullivan. Though Matthew was convinced of his conclusion that the serial killer was still on the loose and that Terry Winters had nothing to do with the four murders, Jason's skepticism nagged at him.

"He's right. There's something he didn't explain." Matthew put on his long jacket and called Mr. Foster to learn whether Terry was with him.

An hour later, Matthew sat with both men in a comfortable living room, had a glass of juice in front of him, and was invited to stay for dinner. He declined politely.

"I'm here for some more questions, Mr. Winters. First, I'm not convinced you panicked at the store. Your explanation for an occasional shoplifting doesn't ring true, and I give you a chance to tell me the truth before I ask for a search warrant for your home and office."

"But I did panic!" Terry took a deep breath. "Not for that special reason, but . . ." He glanced at Harold, and the older man nodded with a smile. "I . . . I was with Harold this morning, and your partner—"

"Agent Beckham, you mean?"

"Yes. He looks like the father of Joshua, one of my kindergarten kids. I was looking against the sun, and the similarity was striking. He—I mean the father—he's a very traditional man, and he would certainly tell the principal . . . about my relationship."

"Why didn't you say so right away? And call your partner to testify?"

"I sensed that Agent Beckham would press on Harold as he pressed on me, if only to make him confirm my alibi right away. I didn't want that to happen. Don't you understand? We went shopping on the other side of town so that we minimized the chance of being seen together. An interrogation at your office would've ruined our secrecy." He ran a hand through his thick hair that fell back across his forehead. "Any . . . questioning by the police might raise suspicion and thus cost me my job. Do you know how hard it is to find a job like this?"

"Still, you made yourself suspicious with this action."

Terry shook his head, looking miserable. "Listen, when my parents died so quickly one after the other, I was devastated. I couldn't work. I wanted to, but every time I left the house I couldn't imagine standing in front of the children, pretending to be the jolly teacher they knew and then break into tears." He fought for composure. "The principal allowed me to take two months off to mourn and take care of the inheritance and the formalities. I'm very grateful that he was so understanding. I kept my job. That means the world to me. Believe me, Agent Montagna, seeing you today turned my world upside down."

"So you assumed Agent Beckham was a father from the kindergarten. Fine. But we identified ourselves. You could've stopped then, but you didn't."

"I can explain that, I think." Mr. Foster took his partner's hand in his as he turned his attention toward Matthew. "I had a very unfriendly encounter with the police in plain clothes a year ago. I was the victim of a mistake — my face looked like that of a robber the police were looking for. I was treated like a criminal — thrown on the sidewalk, frisked, handcuffed, and pushed into the service car. Many people watched the scene, and not a few took a video with their cell phones. You know how this works." He shook his head and adjusted his silver-framed glasses. "The police needed four hours to clear up the mistake and release me. In spite of official statements, a stain remains. People think what they want to think. You can be innocent, but once you're connected to a police investigation, you're in trouble.

"I lost my job that month, though the police gave me a written statement about the mistaken identity. They caught the robber two weeks later. The stain, Agent Montagna, the stain remains. That's why Terry's so sensitive to any appearance of the police, in uniform or not. By the way, he told me that there were police officers in uniform prior to your appearance. Terry was already wondering what they were doing." He gently squeezed Terry's hand. "He's a good man, an honest man. Don't put a stain on his reputation."

Matthew pursed his lips. "Very well. So far, no harm's done aside from the destruction at the store."

"I know. I already sent them a check," Mr. Foster said, and Terry smiled at him thankfully, whereupon Harold tousled his hair.

Matthew couldn't help being touched by the open display of love and was astonished when Terry asked,

"You mentioned a woman who was kidnapped this morning. Did you find her?"

"No, not yet. Our hostage rescue team took over the investigation and is currently waiting for the kidnapper to make contact."

"Do you expect to find her?"

"We hope so." Matthew scrutinized Terry's face, but the kindergarten teacher looked as innocent as any man with blue eyes. In fact, Terry had such an open and friendly expression, Matthew had no doubt he was an excellent teacher. He cleared his throat. "I'm interested in one more thing. Your mother committed suicide eighteen months ago. You stated to the police that she didn't leave a note. Is that true? Do you remember anything odd in her apartment, or was there something in a safe deposit box that you haven't mentioned so far?"

Harold kissed Terry's brow and whispered, "I know it's hard, but you can do this."

Terry nodded, but he spoke as if his throat was constricted. "My parents didn't leave me anything . . . besides clothes, some old pictures, furniture, and some unpaid checks. They weren't rich." He pondered, then sighed. "Listen, Agent Montagna, I was in such a state of shock that I couldn't think clearly." Harold put his arm around Terry's shoulders and hugged him. Once more, Terry's gratefulness showed in his eyes. "I know that she didn't leave a letter for me. No explanation. I assume she couldn't imagine a life without Jim, her husband. He had helped her back into life after her youth had been terrible. He loved and married her, and she always said he was the solid foundation upon which she stood." Terry swallowed and needed a moment to gain his composure. "If you want me to, I can dig into the papers once more, but not right away. Today has held enough unpleasant surprises for me. Thanks to your colleague it was even more unpleasant than it could have been."

Matthew understood the silent scolding, stood, and went to the door. He handed Terry his calling card. "Let me know what you find. Everything is of interest, even though you might not consider it worth mentioning. There's a serial murderer on the loose, and I'm convinced his actions are somehow connected to your mother. I want to catch him."

"Yes, catch some bad guys for a change," Terry said, touching the dressing on his chin.

Matthew wished them a good night and left.

When David had met Rebecca for the first time, she'd been working as a secretary at the body shop where David took his car for repairs. Within five minutes of their conversation, he'd learned of her job competence and her skills with people. Three months later, she'd accepted a job as the secretary of the editor-in-chief of the *Bangor Gazette*. Another two months later, David had seduced her after winning a prize for the best research for a story about a corrupt district attorney. It had been a remarkable night, not only because of the sex, but because she'd appeared to understand his motivation and admired his dedication to the job.

Though David considered himself a good lover, Rebecca demanded that he learn some new positions, practice kissing, and she trained him how to satisfy her with his fingers and lips. She told him to work out to build up his body and gain muscles as well as go for a run at least twice a week. She was a healthy lifestyle activist, and he cherished her values of healthy eating and drinking tea instead of coffee and beer. She organized his spare time, took him to her yoga lessons, and expected him to divide his time well between work and pleasure—a *well-organized work-life-balance*, as she called it. On many occasions, she was bad-tempered when he didn't meet her expectations. Belatedly, David realized that she had turned him into the man she wanted to love.

David chose to rebel against her demands. He rejected her weekly plan and made one of his own. He went to a bar with a friend after hours and had a meeting with his boss when he was supposed to be at the gym. Rebecca scolded him, first quietly but then louder and demanded an explanation. When he told her he wasn't clay she could form as she pleased, she laughed and told him that until he met her, he had been a good reporter but a lousy person.

David didn't like to be criticized, but her words hit home. For two days, he mulled over their argument and whether she was right. He compared his lifestyle to the time prior to meeting her and admitted — grudgingly and only to himself — that Rebecca had improved his life and made him happy. From many interviews, he had learned that the chemistry between a man and a woman was the most important thing in life. More importantly — it was hard to find. David became aware that her manipulation — though obvious — was to his advantage, and he met with her for a chat in one of their favorite health food restaurants.

Instead of gloating over his monologue that she was right and he had become a better person, she kissed him and confessed that she had hoped for him to see the benefits of their relationship.

David was a lucky man. Back then.

Keith was sweating so badly his face was wet. He felt the salty drops trickle down his forehead, cheeks, and along his back. His undershirt as well as his pullover were damp, and though he wanted to run into the woods and catch Mr. and Mrs. Hayes before they were too far away, he had to change clothes. Mumbling words about an impossible escape and that he didn't understand how on earth this could have happened, he packed a backpack with water, food, and ammunition. He left the tranquilizer rifle he had used at the recreation area in his cabin and chose another one with a sight. Stepping out of the cabin, he looked at the sky. He had less time than expected. Quickly, he checked the footprints on the wet soil. The couple had left to the west in order to avoid the direct path toward the road.

"I don't know how they did this," Keith repeated over and over again as he set out with long strides. "It's impossible. They can't fly." He marched with the determination of a man looking for clues.

Though he understood that the couple had walked away, he didn't grasp how they had managed to leave the chamber, and so quickly that he didn't notice their absence immediately. In his mind, he had been away for an hour, but when he checked the sky again, it was getting dark. He could hardly see the ground anymore. Even with a flashlight, the hunt would be difficult.

Frowning, Keith stopped a mile away from his cabin and stood, listening to the sound of the dying wind, of the birds seeking their tree for the night, and the quiet stalking of the nocturnal hunters. Keith wasn't afraid of any predator. He loved to be in the wilderness. Yet he stood unmoving, thinking. He was undecided because a part of him wanted the couple back so that he could ask them the questions nagging him. Another part preferred to go home and eat. He was still hungry, and the image of the many edible things in the refrigerator made his mouth water. The couple would be out there the next day — no one without experience chose a direct path. All the city dwellers and ignorant hikers walked in circles. Keith had seen it before. The people came from cities where they had street signs and streets built like chessboards. Without points for orientation, they were lost.

After fifteen minutes of contemplation, Keith shouldered his rifle and returned to the cabin for a decent supper.

"No matter how I try to forget about it — I'm hungry." Jacky looked at Nicolas, who helped her across a large fallen trunk. The wind had died and the temperature had dropped. It was no longer pleasant to be outdoors.

"Yeah, me, too."

"Oh, right, I forgot — you haven't eaten all day." She looked around. "Is there anything edible at this time of year?"

"Who are you asking? I might be many things, but I'm not a boy scout. I don't have any idea, but if I should guess — it's May. There won't be any berries or nuts ripe for eating."

"You're right."

"Wait. I hear something."

"Traffic on a road?"

"No. Water." Nicolas changed direction and led her through thick underbrush to a small and fast-flowing creek.

She knelt down, sighing with relief.

"Drink slowly," he warned. "It's cold, and your stomach is empty."

"Thanks for the reminder." Jacklyn scooped water with both hands, took a mouthful and swallowed. "It's delicious."

"Water from the mountains." He knelt beside her and drank. His stomach was still rumbling, but he knew he had to drink should they stay in the wilderness for the night. "Down in the city you'd pay three dollars a bottle."

"Having a bottle would be nice."

They drank until they were satisfied. Jacklyn let go of her breath as she lifted her gaze to the darkening sky. "If we weren't on flight from a lunatic —"

"And if we knew where we are going."

"This could be a beautiful trip through Maine's pine

woods. Yes." She kissed his cheek. "But we've got water — at least for the moment — and if it's getting dark now, we should stay close to the creek and have water in the morning."

Nicolas lifted his gaze to the north, farther up a small hill. He squinted as he made it back on his feet, then stood still until the last rays of sunshine were caught in a fragment of glass again.

"Do you see something?" Jacklyn got up. "That looks like someone built a cabin."

"When there's a cabin, there might be someone who owns it. Come." Nicolas reached out for Jacklyn's hand, and they ascended the hill quickly, suddenly light on their feet with the prospect of finding shelter.

Uphill, what they had seen turned out to be the short side of a cabin with a glass mobile hanging from a roof corner. The windows were closed with thick wooden shutters, and the door was locked, too. Nicolas couldn't help but wonder whether both cabins had been built and secured by the same builder.

"Hello? Anybody here?" Nicolas shouted.

He didn't get an answer, even when he shouted again, louder.

"If anyone were here, there would be a car," Jacklyn mused. "Looks like we're alone here." She pulled up her collar, stepping from one foot to the other. "I don't like the idea, either, my lover, but I fear you have to break in."

Nicolas sighed, nodding. "You're right. It doesn't look right for someone like me to invade another person's privacy, but your lips are already blue, and you're shivering constantly. A night in the cold — "

Jacklyn made eyes at him. "I'm the excuse. I'd die here if you don't break in. Just do it."

Behind the cabin, Nicolas found a slim piece of metal he could force between the frame and the shutter and thus crack the lock to take it off. He broke one small window with his elbow and opened the latch. Jacklyn climbed into the house and opened the door from the inside.

"It's a cozy place," she stated. "Still cold, but nice."

It was a comfortable cabin with a living room and a bedroom, a small kitchen, and even a tiny bathroom. There was a generator for electricity, and a propane gas cooking unit. The pictures on the walls showed a couple through the years — in front of a new transporter, in front of a white-painted house with a younger woman in their midst, in a large garden, and with a dog at their side. The interior of the cabin showed female handiwork with homemade quilts on the couch and chairs, a homemade, colorful rug, and decorative pottery that was definitely handmade.

Nicolas covered the broken windowpane with a plank, then collected wood for the fireplace. While he looked in vain for a rifle or any other gun, he found a small, locked room. He suspected the had stowed their guns as the law required, but the door was made of thick wood and locked securely. He had no means to open it and gave up, wondering who the owners might be despite the harmless family pictures. His mind flooded him with information about old serial killer cases, one more brutal than the next. The owners could be criminals or hermits who had decided to leave the civilized world behind. He had no explanation for their security nonsense other than there must be a much-frequented hiking trail close by so that they were afraid of intruders every day. He decided to look for trail signs the next morning.

Jacklyn assessed the provisions and prepared a warm soup. There was no bread, instead zwieback to go with it, and they sat down on the floor in front of the fireplace. The burning logs spread most desired warmth.

Jacklyn sighed after the first spoonful. "It's great that we found shelter. I wonder where the inhabitants are."

He decided not to tell her about the locked door. "Gone to buy provisions, I'd guess. Or they're visiting friends in the next town."

"Whichever it might be." Jacklyn chuckled. "We don't know where we are, but our luck held — we made it out of the trap and into a warm cabin." She reached out for him and gently squeezed his arm. Her hand was still cold. "Thank you, Nick, for taking care of me."

He kissed her lips, feeling grateful for their safety, even though he couldn't shake the thought that the criminal would follow them. The man knew about this cabin for sure, as he would know everything worth knowing about the surrounding woods. If Nicolas and Jacklyn didn't find the road and a driver, they wouldn't get away alive. Nicolas remembered the man's excellent shot from the distance — the single second he had used to mount the muzzle on the passenger door, aim, and shoot. Even Nicolas's drills at Quantico hadn't trained him for such outstanding precision.

He had barred the doorknob with a chair's back, but still he shivered, and it was not from the cold.

Five months ago, David had researched the facts about a wrongfully imprisoned Portland citizen. In the interview David led at his attorney's office, the former prisoner asked whether David had ever been tethered and thus kept from going where he wanted. David said *no*, but when he assembled the details and wove them into a readable text, he tried to imagine how it would be to live in a square cell with a toilet and a sink, eat what the prison cantina served, deal with people you didn't want to know, and be afraid of those who meant you harm. David had taken down the prisoner's story so passionately the man received money and help from all over Maine. Not to mention that the praise and reaction to the story had earned David another star in the chamber of journalistic fame.

While gathering information, David spent more time on the road and with attorneys and human rights activists than with Rebecca. He was the terrier again—he sensed a big story, a scandal, a true tale that had to be told, and bit into it. He didn't stop and take care of his love life. He expected Rebecca to understand his dedication the way she had accepted his way of life at the beginning of their relationship. He called her once a day when he thought of her, but that was it.

Rebecca was dissatisfied, to say the least. Once the story was published and the merits collected, she ordered him to come home.

When he asked what she expected as a suitable compensation, she said with a wicked smile, "You'll do everything I want."

David looked at her, disbelieving his ears. "We're in a relationship. You can't dictate—"

"You'll obey me, or I'll walk through the door and won't come back."

David saw her pursed lips and the threatening glare. He nodded and decided to play along.

David had never betrayed Rebecca. He ogled other women at the paper because he was the top dog *Casanova*, but he didn't do more than flirting, which was fun. Rebecca didn't believe his explanations, claimed that he used the time at work for more than research. Once more she demanded compensation. This time, David had to do the dishes at home, dressed in nothing but a thong. He had to paint her nails and shave her legs wearing nothing for the evening. He thought it was fun for a day, and he could see she was aroused by his actions. When she wanted more, David rethought his compliance.

Rebecca told him he'd better not neglect her ever again or

he would face the consequences. In the following weeks, David pondered her motivation and whether he was a toy for her — and whether he wanted to be her toy for the years to come — if her interest lasted that long. The ensuing arguments about how their relationship should go on led to his attempt at salvaging their love with a wonderful trip through Maine in May. He expected her to be impressed by his plan and that she would fall in love with him all over again.

As he sat in the growing darkness, he yearned for her and the games she invented, still thinking of the horror in her eyes when he last saw her.

"It's a shame we had to break in," Jacklyn whispered as they settled in front of the fireplace with a few quilts and pillows they had found. "I wished we could've asked the owners."

"Me, too." Nicolas fluffed a pillow and pulled the cover close to the fire. He smiled, looking up to her. "And yet, I can hear in your voice that you find this . . . arrangement appealing."

She knelt in front of him and touched his nose with a finger. "Tell me you don't like this part of our adventure. Please, let us forget for a moment — for the night, that we're hunted and that we might not find a way out."

Nicolas kissed her passionately. He wanted the same — forget their predicament, if just for a few hours. He thought of the years they had spent together, of the love they had found even though they didn't seem to fit together at the beginning. Nicolas had never expected an older woman to become the love of his life. And yet Jacklyn offered him everything he ever wanted and then some. Losing her would mean to lose a part of himself.

Their hungry kisses led to fondling and losing clothes. Nicolas hesitated for a moment—it was possible the owners would show up and be more than astonished to find strangers at their home. Then, seeing the longing in Jacklyn's eyes, Nicolas relented. He kissed her inner thighs, inching closer to her vulva, and the sweet scent of her aroused him. He put his hands under her butt cheeks and kneaded her flesh, triggering moans of lust. Jacklyn reached out to caress his member until he was hard. Like flipping a coin, they changed position, and he offered his body for her to worship. As before, she dictated the rhythm, and he was content that Jacklyn got what she wanted. Playfully, she took away his hands from her bosom and pressed them on the cover.

Amid kisses she told him, "You do what I want and you touch me when I grant you permission, Beast."

"Oh, yes, *ma chérie*, oh, yes."

They made love in front of the fire, convincing each other that they were still alive and in love, whatever the dangers of the day to come.

CHAPTER SEVEN

While the sun set and the freezing began, David wondered whether other abducted men like him were tethered to tree trunks and cried for their loved ones.

"Is that what you do, you crazy shithead?" he shouted. "Is that the solution to the riddle of the missing couples? Do you leave the men bound to trunks where no one can find them?" He sobbed. "You're a cruel bastard!" It was such a gruesome image that his stomach churned, and his hunger was forgotten.

As history taught, the really clever killers were never caught. They died or served time in prison for minor offenses. When they got out, they killed again. The man who had kidnapped Rebecca and him was in his late twenties, had shaggy blond hair, narrow eyes, and a cleft lip. He was of average height but strong. His speech was everything but eloquent. David assumed he had hardly finished school and lived most of his life in the wilderness. He knew how to threaten his victims in clipped sentences. In one moment during their interaction, David had believed he had deciphered the man's motivation—when David mentioned his intimate relationship with his mother and told the kidnapper that his mom waited for their return and that she would have a heart attack when he didn't show up with his loved one. The kidnapper had listened intently, nodded once, twice, and hesitated like a man pondering the situation he shared with his victim.

Then the moment was over, and the kidnapper ordered Rebecca and him to climb down the ladder into the chamber.

David shuddered violently thinking of the hours in the ground — locked up without anything, forced to endure hunger and thirst. He had felt like being crushed by the black soil around him. Rebecca's ear-piercing nagging, which led to an open dispute, didn't improve the situation.

Drowning in the misery of his imprisonment, David imagined a creek with flowing water, and from time to time, he heard cars on a road. In the darkness, he cried for help, but no one came. Shivering and self-pitying, he sank into a restless slumber.

"Are you still convinced that Mr. Wonderful good-looking Terry Winters has nothing to do with the murders?" Jason asked as he returned to his desk with a fresh cup of coffee.

Matthew had a hangover from too many late-night beers and wiped his burning eyes. If he ever found a new love, so he swore, he would quit smoking and alcohol at once. So far, his dog didn't mind his mood swings and the stale stench of smoke and beer. He wagged his tail whenever Matthew came home and took care of him. At least the task of taking care of the dog had prevented him from getting completely drunk.

He put his coat on the chair at their desk. "I spoke with both Terry Winters and Harold Foster yesterday before I drove home." He helped himself to a cup of coffee, winking at Jason's angry glare. "I'm still convinced Terry didn't murder the women, but his second explanation — that he was sensitive to police officers of any color because his partner had been wrongfully accused of being a robber — didn't convince me. I found it more convincing when he explained that his partner, Harold, had been at the shop, too, and that you looked like a father of one of the kindergarten kids. They didn't want to be seen together."

"Seriously?" Jason snorted, shook his head, and tilted his cup to empty it. "Then why didn't that partner come forward when we arrested Terry? What a stupid lie."

Matthew exhaled. "I wouldn't call it a lie, but there is something about him that I can't explain, and that's worrying me."

Jason pursed his lips, and the anger in his eyes was getting stronger. "You agree with me, finally, that he has a skeleton in his closet. We don't know yet which kind."

"I can agree to that." Matthew settled on his chair and sipped coffee. As usual, Jason had brewed an excellent brand. He would never admit it, but Matthew was addicted to the expensive stuff. "Both men exerted themselves convincing me of their story and that their relationship must remain a secret because of Terry's job." He smacked his lips. Now that the caffeine kicked in, his headache abated. "Something is odd about Terry."

Jason huffed. "Oh, seriously?"

"Him living in a gay partnership doesn't make him a crime suspect per se. All right? Drop that act."

Jason added a drop of milk to his coffee, pouting like a girl. "What's your next step?"

Matthew was astonished his partner had asked. "I'll put Terry under surveillance. He might not be the murderer, but he might have a connection to him we don't see yet."

"Wise decision."

Matthew didn't like Jason's mocking tone, but decided to drop the subject. "Have you heard from Nick?"

"Not a word, but that was the plan. They want to have some time off and not hear about cases."

Matthew kept back a smile. Whenever Nicolas Hayes was off duty, both Jason Beckham and the CSU agent in charge, Dr. Miller, acted as if they were missing a body part. It was fun to watch how their faces dropped when Nicolas was mentioned and how their yearning affected their work. Matthew decided to ask Nicolas upon his return whether he might want to open a fan club.

David got to his feet, shuddering so violently his teeth clattered. He relieved himself and when he was dressed again started jumping jacks to warm up as best as he could. The first ones were the worst—his body was stiff from another night on the cold leaves, and a part of him argued it was meaningless whether he moved or not. He would die anyway and it just prolonged his suffering. He was already weak.

Then there was the terrier in him—the person that clung to every bit of information, hunted for witnesses and informants, and presented a well-researched story that stunned his editor-in-chief as well as readers. He didn't want to let go of his life when there was a chance to survive and write the story himself and earn the merits for his suffering. He envisioned walking up the podium slowly—still recovering from his energy-sapping adventure—and being handed the *Pulitzer Prize* for the best story of the year. The head of the jury would laude him for solving the serial killer case and surviving the killer's devilish intention of letting him die slowly.

He went on jumping up and down, clinging to the thought of being saved and writing what no other reporter could write. He wished he had paper and pencil with him to write a diary about his days in the wilderness, equipped with nothing but a bottle of water.

He stopped jumping when reality caught up with him. He had little water left, and there was no chance to find food in the eight-foot radius around the tree. He had already tried to eat leaves and spat them out. They were bitter and, maybe poisonous. He tried worms but there were few, and his stomach churned thinking about dirty stuff that lived in the soil. He assumed that his hunger would grow to a degree he didn't mind eating grass and worms and whatever beetle came his way, but he wasn't down to that yet.

He drank a sip of water and screwed the bottle carefully. Even in tiny rations, it wouldn't last longer than a day. Then thirst would add to the nagging hunger. David sat down at the tree again and wiped his dirty face.

"Think of the story of your life," he whispered. "You must write it, for no other reporter can do this." Trying to regain his composure, David looked up at the brightening sky of yet another morning. It was sunny, and with luck, temperatures would rise into the low sixties. "Here you are, in bumfuck country, with nothing but your wits and half a bottle of water." He looked at the cuff around his ankle where the skin was abraded and inflamed. Tears trickled down his cheeks. "What do you do?"

Nicolas disentangled from Jacklyn's embrace when he heard noise outside the cabin.

"Wake up! I think we're getting company."

Jacklyn was awake from one moment to the next and grabbed her clothes. Nicolas got dressed in pants and undershirt and ran for the door right before the key was put in the lock. He took away the chair and opened the door. "Good morning."

A gray-haired woman, short and round like an old teapot, stared at him, flabbergasted. Stepping back, she put a hand on her bosom. "Oh, my god! Who are you?"

The man behind her, taller but no less corpulent around the middle, stopped a step away from the threshold. His jaw sagged, and his eyes widened with the greatest disbelief Nicolas had ever seen in a comedy. If it wasn't for the severity of their situation, he would have laughed and opened his arms wide. Nicolas stepped backward to grant them room.

He lifted his hands to show he was unarmed. "I'm sorry that we—"

"Who the hell are you?" the man asked in a harsh, dark voice. "How do you dare break into our home?"

"And make yourself comfortable with our belongings!" she said, pointing at the covers and pillows. "Are you out of your mind?"

She made a step forward, and Nicolas tried to find words to soothe them. He expected the man to pull a gun any moment and readied to protect Jacklyn.

"Please, listen," Jacklyn said, getting up. He didn't know how she had done it, but she was fully dressed. "We are really, truly sorry we had to invade your home, but—"

"You'd better show some respect for other people's possessions!" The woman checked the living room quickly, angry beyond belief. "You're terrorists, that's what you are!"

"Not really." Nicolas kept the man in view, tense like a bowstring. He wouldn't start a confrontation, but if a gun was in play, he'd go for it. "We had no choice. We needed shelter for the night or would've frozen."

"And we were hungry." Jacklyn smiled apologetically. "We wished you had been here to help us. I know you are kind people who wouldn't have let us starve."

"As I see you made good use of our provisions."

The woman tore off her hat and threw it on the table. Furiously, she turned to face Jacklyn, and Nicolas redirected. Maybe the woman was more dangerous than the man.

"How dare you?"

"We'll pay you back." Jacklyn folded the covers and put the pillows on the couch. "Please, understand our situation. We were—"

"We got lost in the woods," Nicolas interrupted and signaled her with a glance to stop talking. "We walked and walked, and suddenly we were lost and didn't find our way back to our car. Stupid, huh?"

"Very stupid. Dudes!"

"I'm Nick, and that's my fiancé, Jacklyn." He reached out, but the woman didn't take his hand. He dropped his. "And you are?"

"I hope you didn't break anything."

"We didn't. Believe us, please, we did this because we were in dire need. It's not our habit to break into other people's homes." Nicolas observed the exchange of glances between the couple. They didn't like having strangers on their premises. He couldn't blame them. He wouldn't want to come home and find their house occupied by strangers, who had plundered the fridge.

"I'm Joe, and this is my wife, Veronica. Where are you guys from?" Joe put down a basket on the floor, still eyeing their visitors.

Nicolas concluded the couple wasn't armed. Otherwise they would both be in the crosshairs by now. Quickly, he took the pullover Jacklyn handed him and put on his socks and boots. "We're on vacation. We traveled from Portland."

"Ah, Portland," Joe said, nodding. "I like that city."

Veronica took the covers and the pillows toward the bedroom, glancing over her shoulder. "I like when people go to a hotel for the night."

"We would've done that." Jacklyn smiled amiably. She reached for her coat. "But we couldn't. Is it far to the main road?"

"Quite some miles, yes. And not really" —Joe looked at Jacklyn's pretty boots—"meant for city people with shoes meant for a nicely paved sidewalk." He put the basket on the table and went back to their pickup truck to fetch one more.

"Could we ask you to take us there? Then you'd be rid of us right away."

Jacklyn looked at Nicolas, but he had no idea how to convince the couple to give them a lift. He recalled that settlers like Joe and Veronica were friendly and helpful to strangers. These two looked like they would rather bite than give them a hand.

"Car's broke," Joe grumbled. "We hardly made it here."

"What's broken? Maybe I can help." Nicolas tried to make eye contact, but Joe shook his head and unpacked the baskets.

"Tire's almost flat. And the other one we've got needs some air, too. Sorry, young man, no help from this side."

Nicolas swore he saw glee in the man's eyes. His behavior added to the confusion of what he had expected and what was actually happening. A small voice in his mind told him to get away. As unobtrusively as possible, he checked the tire by a glance through the window. Joe was right—the old pickup's right front tire was losing air. Nicolas slipped into his long jacket. "Maybe you could be so kind as to give us some food and water and show us the direction to the road. We can make it, I think."

"You'd get lost again." Veronica returned, her anger obviously mellowed now that she found out that the strangers had indeed treated her possessions with care. Her voice lost the accusing edge. "You'd only have a chance with a guide. There are no street signs around her, you know." She huffed again as she went to the kitchenette and put a kettle on the hot plate. "We won't do it, don't ask for that. But Joe can call for help." She shrugged, and her gaze was condescending. "I wouldn't want you to run in circles and strand at our door again."

"That would be kind. You have a phone up here in the wilderness?"

"No." Veronica shot him another glance while Joe laughed aloud. "But we do have a radio."

"Could you call the sheriff for us?" Jacklyn asked before Nicolas could stop her.

"The sheriff?" Joe stopped unpacking the groceries to stare at Jacklyn, then at Nicolas. His jowls sagged like that of a basset. He frowned deeply. "There's no reason to call him. No crime has been committed. You got lost. That's all." He shrugged. "I'll call my nephew. That'll do. So, you can help set the table or at least don't stand in the way."

"Your nephew?" Jacklyn asked. Nicolas heard the terror in her voice. "Does he live in these woods, too?"

"No, in Bangor, silly. That's why calling him for help makes such a lot of sense!" Veronica poured hot water into two cups. "Are you two not just terrorists, but stupid, too? Of course, he lives here. Unlike my ungrateful daughter, he appreciates life out here. He grew up to become a master of the woods." For the first time, Veronica smiled. "He's a good man. He tells us that he helps people in need all the time. You know, when they have a flat or their car won't start again. He knows a lot about engines. He's a very helpful person, more than you deserve. He'll take you to town." She inclined her head, looking at Joe, who was already unlocking the door to the small room.

Nicolas locked gazes with Jacklyn, and she urged him to do something.

"I'd really prefer you to call the sheriff, ma'am. That would spare your nephew the hassle to come here."

"He has to help us with the tires, anyway. And the sheriff's a day out." Veronica looked up while stirring sugar into her tea. "Are you trying to tell me something? Do you want to confess another crime than burglary? I'd appreciate that."

"Where are we? What's the next town?"

"Byron." She blew over her tea, still eyeing Nicolas distrustfully in an alarming way. "But we're miles off the main road. This isn't New York, huh?"

"No, it's not."

"Where did you leave the car?" Veronica asked. "On which

road?"

Nicolas looked back at the half-open door. He heard Joe talk with someone, but couldn't make out words. His stomach tightened.

"Ma'am . . . I really don't want you to get in trouble, but we had an encounter with someone not so nice." Once more, he gazed at the door. Joe was still talking amiably with someone on the other end of the line. "But we were chased and —"

"Because you broke into another man's home?" Veronica shook her head, and the anger was back in her voice. "You're both criminals, right? You run around, try to find something of value and move on. If you get caught, you pretend you were in dire need so that everyone consoles you. But you're wrong. I want your names and address, and I want you to pay for what you took here. Including the broken window."

"We will, but we don't have money with us. We were —"

"Oh, seriously?" Veronica slammed the cup on the table so that tea spilled on the tablecloth. Her eyes narrowed as her nostrils flared. The accusing tone was back. "Now you're claiming that you got robbed and don't have money with you? You, a rich couple from the city, who probably came here with an eighty-thousand dollars car. Is that what you're trying to tell me?" She scoffed. "Yeah, just what I thought."

Joe reappeared, smiling broadly. "Keith is coming right away. He has a spare tire. Can you imagine that? He kept it from an old car. Sometimes I wonder whether he has a shed full of tires and motor parts. He could open a body shop."

"That's good news. He's a very handy young man — knows how to repair a lot of stuff." Veronica stared at Jacklyn. "Until then, keep her in check, and he's to write a list of what he'll repay us."

"All right." Joe made a move, and Nicolas realized that he had been played.

Once more, Jacklyn was looking into the muzzle of a gun.

David had tried to push the chain up the tree trunk so that he might climb into the lowest branches and have an overview. Maybe he would see where he was—if there was a road downhill, but the chain was wound too tight. He couldn't even move it horizontally around the tree to have more leeway. He was trapped for good, and his despair grew with every passing hour.

He wanted Rebecca in his arms again. Worrying about her fate suppressed his fear of death for a while. He wanted to hold her again, smell her scent, touch her hair, kiss her lips. He couldn't stomach that their last few minutes together had been filled with an argument about his intention on the trip.

Rebecca had stood in front of him in the earth chamber, crying her eyes out.

Then the kidnapper pulled out the ladder and locked the grating.

They had nowhere to go. Suddenly, as if their situation wasn't bad enough, Rebecca pounded David's chest and screamed at him.

"You miserable bugger! This has been your plan from the beginning, right? That's why we you rented such a fucking big car at the airport! That's why you wanted to drive on side roads instead of the interstate. It was your plan all along to get this killer's attention. Are you out of your fucking mind? You're playing with our lives here! Do you want to die? Because I don't!"

David tried to soothe her, but he couldn't find words to cloak what was so damn obvious. Unlike in the movies, she didn't relent in his arms so he could hold her while she cried.

"You don't love me, do you?" Rebecca slapped him in the

face. "You only love your stories, your fame, and your god-damn money! Shit! You're such a sucker!"

David held his cheek. She had hit him hard, and the sting went deep. When he looked up, the killer stared at him, his mouth agape and saliva trickling from his lower lip.

"You don't love her."

It was a statement that chilled David to the bone. He knew instantly he had made a big mistake. The killer looked at Rebecca. Her face was contorted with anger, and their kidnapper frowned as if the situation was so new and unexpected that he had no concept of how to deal with it.

"This was made up." The killer changed his attention to David. He spoke slowly with more astonishment than anger. "*You* made this up."

David shook his head, sensing the imminent danger. "No! I do love her! I took her on a vacation. This wasn't meant to be. You ruined this!"

But the killer repeated his words over and again. He walked off, then came back and opened the grating to shove down the ladder. Still looking confused, he pointed a gun at David.

"You, woman, climb out. You don't have to be here."

Rebecca stood in shock, numbed by the prospect of yet another misery. "What about him?" she asked.

"He doesn't love you. Get out, or I'll shoot you both. Right here. You are no couple. You hate each other."

"No, don't take her away!" David shouted. "I love her!"

"Get out!" the killer repeated. "Or die."

Rebecca looked at David, tears in her eyes, biting her lips. "You brought us here, into this shit. I'm sorry, but I don't wanna die in this hole."

David was stunned that she'd left him. His heart beat in his throat, and he didn't find the right words to tell her that the killer wouldn't escort her back to Portland so that she might fly back to Bangor. She would end up in a shallow grave somewhere in these goddamned woods.

She climbed the ladder, and the killer grabbed her arm and pulled her out to push her aside. She cried out in pain.

"Rebecca!" David looked up while the killer retrieved the ladder. "Don't take her away from me, you beast!" He tried to hold on to the ladder but let go when the gun was pointed at him. The killer dragged the ladder out and crashed it on the ground.

"You don't love her." The killer locked the chamber again, and for a second, David saw Rebecca's horrified face as the killer grabbed her forcefully, shoved the gun at her head, and grunted, "You don't deserve her."

David feared he would pull the trigger and make him watch her die. "No! No! Don't hurt her!"

Rebecca cried out again when the kidnapper dragged her across the yard. David screamed her name again and again, to no avail. Then the sounds abated, and David heard the engine of the criminal's old van start. A moment later, the van was gone and David alone without knowing whether the killer would come back.

David shivered violently. The hours in the semi-darkness had been filled with lasting despair that he was meant to die slowly, without anyone knowing of his whereabouts. He would suffer thirst, hunger, pain, and cold until he lost consciousness. Later, the killer would pull out his dead body to let it rot somewhere. Rebecca would be killed elsewhere, and he cried for her premature death, too. He had been honest—he loved her with all his heart.

However, writing stories was his job, his passion that he loved with equal intensity. He couldn't breathe without thinking about the next headline. If he wanted anything in life, it was the chance to uncover the truth and tell it to the readers.

Covering his face with his hands, David cried out his misery.

CHAPTER EIGHT

Nicolas stretched out his hands while he moved in front of Jacklyn, keeping an eye on Joe. "That's a very old gun, sir. Don't shoot us by accident." He pulled Jacklyn behind him while he tried to keep Veronica in view. "Keith kidnapped us on the road to Popeville and put us in a hole in the ground."

Joe pointed the timeworn rifle at Nicolas's belly. "You're making this up!" the old man said angrily. "Liars! Both of you! You'll stay until Keith gets here. He will clear this up. He's got some really valuable things at his cabin. Maybe you broke into his home, too, and are now searching for a way to get out of this!"

"No, that's not what we did!" Nicolas moved to the side slowly and took Jacklyn with him so that the front door was at their backs. "You're right, we're a rich couple from the city, but not Portland. We're on vacation from Washington, DC. It's our first vacation in years, and we wanted to spend some days in Popeville when a young man with shaggy blond hair stunned my fiancé and shot me with an arrow. He locked us up in a hole in the ground and—"

"Stop telling nonsense! Popeville is a two-hour drive from here!" Veronica shouted. "You broke into our home, and I bet you broke into his, too! What's that stupid story about arrows?" She shook her head that her gray hair loosened from the bun and fell down on her shoulders. "You rich people think you can go anywhere, do what you want, and get away with it. Always!"

"Please, put down the gun. I'm unarmed, and I don't want to hurt you. All that we want is to go back to the city."

"You committed a crime, mister." Joe sounded like one of the old judges in a western movie. "And we'll make sure that you pay for it."

Jacklyn piped up from behind Nicolas's back. "That man — is that Keith?"

"Our nephew would never chase and hurt anyone. He's a good man. Friendly. Helpful. He doesn't do harm to anyone."

Nicolas realized that it was Keith's strategy to stop for people in need and carry them off. He had built the chamber in the ground to keep his victims from running while he arranged for their deaths.

Jacklyn pressed her nails into his sides, breathing shallowly. When he touched her hands, he felt her trembling. He loosened her grip and signaled her by tugging her shirt she should be ready to drop to the floor. She whispered "okay," only for him to hear.

"We've got nowhere to go," Nicolas said hoping to calm the situation. "And we will repay you the damage we caused, but, please, lower the gun. The way you hold it, I might get shot by accident."

Joe cocked his head, looking sly. "You think you city dwellers know better about my gun than I do? Idiot!" He looked at his wife. "I guess you'd better find some rope to tie them up. I don't —"

Within the second of inattention, Nicolas bridged the distance.

"Watch out!" Veronica shouted.

Joe pulled up the gun, eyes wide with surprise. He pulled the trigger unintentionally, and the bang stunned Nicolas's hearing. Joe made a step backward, but then Nicolas held tight to the barrel and tore the gun out of Joe's hands. He clubbed the old man with the butt on the head, and Joe collapsed, unconscious.

"Turn around!" Jacklyn shouted in terror.

Nicolas swiveled around, the rifle still held like a club, to see Veronica attacking him with a kitchen knife.

"You fucking murderer!" she screamed.

Nicolas reacted instinctively and hit Veronica's arm holding the knife. The woman cried out in pain, but didn't let go. Instead, she attacked him again with more force, baring her teeth. Nicolas saw no other way than to disarm and hit her hard enough that she stumbled against the table. Her knees buckled, and she sat on the floor, staring up at him with more hatred than he had expected to see in a woman. Her cheek reddened immediately, and she had tears in her eyes.

"Give up!" he boomed.

Veronica panted heavily, but her look was filled with hatred.

Nicolas didn't expect her to listen to reason. He remained in a fighting stance. His voice was hoarse. "Get me a rope so we can tie them up."

Jacklyn went looking in the small kitchen and handed him a coil that she found under the cooking plate inside a cupboard.

"Your arm's bleeding," Jacklyn said meekly.

"Are you okay?" Nicolas had trouble hearing, but the adrenalin in his blood sharpened his other senses. He looked her up and down and didn't find any injuries.

"I'm fine."

She looked shaken and afraid, but he had no time to console her. He bound Veronica's and Joe's hands behind their backs.

"Keith will find you, I'm sure of that," he said when Veronica spat curses at him. "Jacky, find a backpack, water bottles, some food to take with us. Hurry! Keith is already on his way." He turned to search the small room with the radio, but didn't find any other weapon than the old rifle. Though he had a box with ammunition, a closer look at the bolt and the bolt handle revealed the rifle could blow into the next man's face. The parts were old and loose. He put it aside.

"No more guns?" Jacklyn asked when she stuffed zwie-back, cookies, and a large piece of cheese into the backpack. "Do we have to run?" She added four small bottles of water.

"Without proper guns we can't risk staying."

"The radio?"

"He has rendered it useless."

Veronica huffed. "You think he'd leave it for you? No dice." She spat out. "You're killers! First, you invade our home, and now you've killed my husband!"

"He's not dead," Jacklyn replied. "But he left us no choice."

"It was *your* choice to rob us in the first place. My nephew is right — all of you rich people are arrogant, stupid brats, who should stay away from the woods. You're nothing but free-loaders, neither fit nor worth to survive!" She spat at Jacklyn.

Nicolas silenced Jacklyn with a glance. There was no use in talking to Veronica. She had made up her mind and would not listen to reason. He thought about the family connections and whether the couple knew of Keith's crimes. If so, Nicolas had to take Jacklyn as far away as possible, or they'd have three people on their heels. The image of Keith hunting them through the woods sent a cold shiver down his spine.

"I packed what I could. Now let me have a look at the wound."

"Jacklyn, no." He evaded her attempt to part him with his long jacket. "We don't have time. If you find a first aid kit, take it with you, but in any other case — let's go."

"All right." She went to the bathroom and collected a pair of scissors and dressing material. Jacklyn handed him the backpack. "Are we leaving them like this?" She went for the door.

"Yes. Let me go first." He took the knife from the floor, buttoned his long jacket, and shouldered the backpack, grimacing at the sudden pain in his shoulder muscles. When he looked out through the window, he expected to look into the muzzle of Keith's tranquilizer gun, but he couldn't make out any movement in the woods. By now, the pickup's tire was flat so that the vehicle tilted to the side.

They left the cabin behind, and he took Jacklyn's hand.

"The same procedure?" she asked quietly as they left the path the pickup had taken to the left and started through the underbrush.

"Yes, the same procedure. If we follow the path, we'll meet Keith faster than we want to."

"I don't want to meet anyone. I'm sick of people."

"I know."

"Are you okay? The wound —"

"Later. Veronica will tell Keith when we left. We don't have time."

"But I don't want you to collapse. It's a miracle that you're still running."

Nicolas smiled at her lopsidedly as he set out with long strides, pulling her with him. "It's the FBI code to never let a civilian see that you are in pain."

"But —"

"Hurry, Jacky, the more distance we put between him and us the better."

Keith turned off the radio and sat on the small three-legged stool in front of it, trying to grasp what his uncle had told him. He chewed on a bagel with cream cheese and slurped milk from the bottle.

"Hayes?" he said aloud. "They made it to Aunt Ronnie and

Uncle Joe? How?"

After the various encounters he had experienced, he didn't consider it possible that city dwellers knew how to find their way through the woods. It was close to a miracle they had found Uncle Joe's cabin and managed to break in. In a crude way, Keith was grateful the couple had made it this far. Now he knew where to drive.

After dinner the day before, Keith had decided to get up at dawn and hunt the Hayeses as fast as he could. Now he was glad he had slept in.

Outside, he remembered the van cutting out the day before and stopped to decide whether it was wise to repair the car first or pay his relatives a visit. He decided to load the tires for Joe's pickup truck and take the risk of driving. He added his backpack and his best rifle and set out.

During the ride, he thought about his parents and their attempts at improving their lives — their marriage, their small laundromat, their living conditions. However, every time Keith had thought his parents would make it, his father had drowned his mind in booze, played the silly good-for-nothing, and angered his wife to a degree that bordered on madness. While his father's outbreaks had held a kind of amusement for a small kid, it was no longer funny for a teenager, who understood the meaning of money and suffered the effect of its lack.

Keith spent his younger years in fear that the family had no money, no car, no place to stay. It wasn't because the laundromat didn't work, it was because his father paid too much for the rotgut he said he needed to think clearly. One day, when Jeffrey was rat assed but still able to hold a club, he hit Keith so hard that he slumped against the kitchen table, bleeding from his nose and mouth. The next moment, when Keith looked up, his mother had leveled the rifle and fired a single shot. Jeffrey went down like a stone, a bullet hole in his chest.

Keith remembered his mother's purposeful look that held neither shame nor remorse. She claimed she had done what was necessary to rid the world of a loser, and then she ordered Keith to help her take the body deep into the woods to bury him.

Keith didn't say a word—not about his dead father, not about her taking justice into her own hands, or that she wouldn't call the sheriff. He helped her as best as he could, and they dug a hole in the ground while she made up a reasonable story to explain Jeffrey's disappearance. A year later, she went to the authorities and claimed that her husband had left her and was gone without a trace. She took back her maiden name because she wanted to wipe out everything that reminded her of Jeffrey's presence in her life.

Her mother's cleverness helped them survive, helped them prosper and rely on the income of the laundromat. Though they lived hand-to-mouth for several months, they didn't need to share the money with an addict anymore.

Keith's life improved and was stable until his mother's brutal death fifteen months earlier.

Matthew put down the receiver and hesitated to reveal the contents of the call to Jason, who sat at the opposite desk, skimming through papers. He knew it was wrong to keep back information, but due to Jason's reaction the other day, he had a gut feeling that taking his partner on the ride would be hazardous.

He stood and put on his jacket. "I'll have a chat with—"

Jason dropped the pen on the pages and leaned back in his chair. His look was adamant. "You got a call from the surveillance team. Anything worth knowing?"

Matthew didn't need profiler skills to read Jason's expression. "All right, yes, I got new information about Terry Winters. But before you say *I knew it*, let us talk with him like civilized agents, all right? He's not been accused of a crime."

"Yet." Jason buttoned his trench coat—his latest acquisition—and took the keys to their service car. "What did your man say?"

Out of the corner of his eye, Matthew detected Senior Agent Sullivan at the door of his office. He signaled them to come in.

"And now we're off to a new browbeating," Jason murmured as they changed direction. "Did you send your report yesterday?"

"I did."

They entered Sullivan's spick-and-span office that was bare of any knickknacks normal people usually displayed in their offices.

Sullivan ordered them to have a seat. "I received a call from the bureau in Portland. It appears that Agent Hayes and Mrs. Hollander are reported missing."

"What?" Jason gaped at his superior. "What happened?"

"If you don't interrupt me, I can tell you." Sullivan paused to look at Jason like a stern father, then went on. "Their rental car was found outside of Portland on a side road. The key was in the ignition, Mrs. Hollander's purse on the passenger seat. The investigation brought forth that another car, probably a van, parked in front of the SUV and that Agent Hayes and Mrs. Hollander were dragged inside that vehicle. His fingerprints are on the hood of the SUV but no others. There are no traffic cams or any other surveillance gear, so the agents in Portland cannot tell anything about the kidnapper—or more than one—or the couple's current whereabouts."

Matthew sat as if he had been hit in the gut. He ran a hand across his beard and tried to focus on the fact that Sullivan considered the couple kidnapped not murdered.

"But Nick wouldn't go down without a fight. Any signs of that?" Jason's face had lost all color, and his voice betrayed his worry.

Agent Sullivan pretended he didn't hear the question. "As it turns out, the kidnapping of my agent and Mrs. Hollander wasn't the first one committed in western Maine. The FBI division tasked with the investigation calls him the *MCK*, the *Maine Couple Killer*. Not inventive but fitting. There have been eight more couples gone missing within thirteen months. While their rental cars were located, none of the couples were found. They're gone without a trace."

"No one disappears without a trace," Matthew said quietly. "Do they know anything about the kidnapper or a reason why the criminal started kidnapping people?"

"I asked for a copy of their file but haven't received it yet." Sullivan cleared his throat. "If I hear any news, I'll keep you informed."

"I want to join the search," Jason said spontaneously. "You could send me to Portland to support the team."

Sullivan's brows would've touched his hairline if they could. "I won't do any such thing. You have a pile of cases on your table, and none of them are solved. I recommend dealing with them first before you ask for work in Portland."

"But, sir—"

"Dismissed."

Matthew got up and cleared his throat. When Jason exchanged glances with him, Matthew inclined his head toward the door. Outside the office, Jason's shoulders sagged, and he wiped his face as they walked to the parking lot.

Despite their differences, Matthew pitied his partner. "The FBI up there has a good team. They'll find them."

"Nine couples, Matt! That's eighteen people missing somewhere without a trace! Thirteen months and no clue. What does that tell you about the agents' rate of success?" Jason fumbled for the keys and dropped them beside the driver's door.

Matthew picked them up. "I'll drive." When Jason didn't protest, Matthew knew his partner was devastated. He sat behind the wheel and waited.

Jason rounded the hood, then turned away from the car and stood for a minute, unmoving. Matthew saw his shoulders heave as he fought and lost his composure. When Jason settled in the passenger seat, Matthew started the engine and didn't comment on his partner wiping a tear from the corner of his eye. "Sullivan's an asshole. He could've told us the news later in the day."

Jason stared through the windshield. "Tell me about the surveillance team."

Matthew nodded as he steered the car into the morning traffic. "The man they were monitoring was seen entering a large business building for unknown reasons, and after that he met with a stranger in a dark alley — a place where no facial recognition would work. The agents didn't see who it was, and when they pursued him, the stranger lost them within five minutes." He glanced at Jason. "As if he knew he was being followed."

Jason took a deep breath. "Let's talk with Mr. Winters once more." While Matthew knew the day before he would have been happy to pick on Terry, Jason's voice sounded tired and resigned.

Rebecca had taught David it was healthy to drink at least half a gallon of water and tea a day. David laughed bitterly as he drained the small bottle of water he had rationed through two and a half days. At nightfall, he would be hungry, thirsty, and cold — more miserable than anything thus far yet. His will to survive still flickered, but his hopes diminished. He wasn't the tough type of guy who could endure deprivation and laugh about it.

He had been raised in the city with many home comforts. Never before had he suffered and yearned for such simple things like water and a piece of bread. Thinking of food worsened the stomach cramps.

When the kidnapper had returned after long hours, David had cried to be released. Instead, the goon had worked on his car. Judging by the sounds, David assumed he was changing the set of tires. After that, he had gone into his house and not returned for another hour. David was mad about waiting for anything, even if it was something bad to happen.

Later that afternoon, the kidnapper had ordered him to leave the hole, pointing a gun at him and retreating quickly enough so that David had no chance to attack him. The criminal pointed at a small glass on the ground. "Drink this."

"You're gonna poison me? Now, after letting me suffer with thirst and hunger?" David had smelled bacon in the air and been close to throttling his kidnapper, in spite of the risk of being shot. "What's this all about? And where did you take Rebecca?"

"Drink this."

David had howled in despair, but seen no other choice if he didn't want to be shot. Haltingly, he'd emptied the glass. The clear liquid had tasted like a kind of medicine, and the effect had been immediate. He had fallen on his knees, and his vision blurred. Heart beating in his throat, he had heard the kidnapper stow his gun. David had tried to find the courage to do something—maybe topple the guy into the hole and escape. The weakness in his limbs had been terrifying—he had the dreadful image of being permanently paralyzed. Who knew what went on in this crazy shithead's mind?

The kidnapper had dragged him toward the van, tied his

hands behind his back with zip ties, and thrown him in the cargo area. David had remained conscious, but couldn't yell or move around, let alone push open the rear doors. He'd felt like a Kafka-esque beetle on its back—hearing it all, seeing it all, but unable to change his fate.

The van had rumbled across uneven paths, across rocks or roots and branches, so David had assumed the kidnapper was driving cross-country. He was shaken, lost consciousness when he'd hit his head, and woke up when the kidnapper opened the rear doors and dragged him out.

"Walk!"

David had seen the long chain in the man's hands and tried to bargain, but he couldn't convince the stupid man to let him go, no matter what reward David offered. He'd pleaded for his life and how cruel it was to be left in the wilderness. He'd been stunned when the kidnapper chained him to the tree and cast him a water bottle.

"Where's Rebecca?" David had shouted when the man cut the zip tie and turned away, folding his knife.

"In a better place."

David hadn't wanted to read between the lines that his loved one was dead. "Did you kill her?"

"She's in a better place," the criminal had repeated and walked away, disregarding David's attempts at getting another answer.

He still hoped against hope that the euphemism did not mean the goon had killed her, though a part of him called himself a dreamer. Killing was the man's main task. He had kidnapped and murdered fourteen people and wouldn't stop. David couldn't believe that Rebecca of all people had escaped that monster's viciousness.

CHAPTER NINE

M atthew glanced at Jason now and then, hoping he was inobtrusive, but he needed to know about his partner's mental condition. It wasn't wise — not in the light of Jason's homophobia — to take him to an interrogation with someone who might or might not be involved in a crime.

"I'll stay in the background," Jason said quietly as they left the car at the curb. "Don't worry that I'll throttle Mr. Winters on the spur of the moment."

"Jason, I—"

"Don't offer to question him alone. I'm a professional. I can handle missing partners and gay men with a suspicious history." He straightened the cuffs of his dress shirt while Matthew pushed the doorbell. "Let me play the threat in the background. Maybe that will work."

"You're saying I'm too nice?" Matthew smiled lopsidedly. "Yeah, sometimes."

"I'm saying that I want to throttle a liar and thus blow off steam because I can't kill the bastard who has kidnapped my friends."

Matthew raised his brows, but didn't dare say a word.

"*What*, Matthew?" Jason kept him from entering the building. "Is it so unusual that I'm worried for my best friend's whereabouts? I know he's a capable agent, but maybe he's met a capable criminal. And he has Jacklyn with him, which means he'll stop the world from turning if it will keep her safe. It means he'll put himself in the line of fire and not stop when he's threatened."

105

"You're right. He'll do whatever it takes to keep her out of harm's way."

"It's not reassuring that this asshole of a kidnapper was able to displace eighteen people so far. What's his MO? How is it possible that roadblocks and searches were in vain? How can he disappear with two people in his van, truck, or a camper without being watched? Not once!"

"Can we continue this discussion later? I'd like to talk to Terry Winters once more."

"Right." Jason stared at his shoes for a moment, then nodded, and faked a smile. "Ready when you are."

Terry's face fell upon seeing Jason entering the apartment behind Matthew.

"Another interrogation, this time cloaked as a friendly conversation?" the young man asked after he offered them seats in the living room. As it turned out, Harold was not at home. In the background, piano music was playing. In the center of the room stood an ironing table, and several dress shirts hung on hangers close by, some of them ironed to perfection. "I looked through my parents' papers and belongings—the few I kept—but I didn't find anything of interest. They had only a few friends and didn't go on vacation." Terry sat down on the couch opposite Jason and Matthew and pulled up his legs. "My mother was ashamed of her looks and didn't like being around people."

"Mr. Winters, we know that your mother attended high school and was friends with five other women. If the information can be trusted, they spent a lot of time together." Matthew watched Terry's expression carefully. So far, the young man looked interested but not alarmed. "Your mother had a car accident when she was eighteen years old—the one that left her face partially paralyzed. We know from school records that she didn't go back to high school. Did she stay in contact with her friends? Do you have any knowledge of the events after she left the hospital? Did she ever talk with you about her friends or what happened back in those days?"

Terry Winters kneaded his hands. His face twitched, and when he wet his lips, he appeared close to crying. "I can't fathom how she must have felt — eighteen! And disfigured for life. Whenever she mentioned the year after the accident, she was . . . bitter, disappointed, and always crying. She repeated she wished that circumstances had been different and that she would have loved to have another choice. You should know, my mother had no relatives besides an aunt, who didn't truly love her and had no money to support her. Her mom had died when she was eight, and her father was so grief-stricken he didn't want to keep her with him. My mother had to deal with the injuries and the tragedy of being ugly alone. Her friends turned away from her. Imagine that! One week they went everywhere together, and the next one they didn't talk with her anymore. When she needed them most, they dropped her."

"Do you know why she was shunned?"

Terry wiped his hands on his sweat pants. "No. She told me she'd been depressive and thought about committing suicide back then. Maybe that was why she broke off with them. Or they broke off with her. I can't tell." He wiped his face, looking sad, as if he were back in time with his young mother. "She admitted that she took drugs, but they only numbed her senses for a while. The situation got worse when her aunt told her to leave the house. She didn't want a junkie around."

Terry sipped from a small glass of alcohol. If Matthew had to guess, it was a fruit liqueur. His stomach churned, and he longed for a beer.

"When she took her belongings to live in a shelter for a while, she met my father. He was a social worker at that time and had recently started his duties at the facility." Terry nodded toward the glass on the small table. "Without him — I don't know what would've happened to her. But he listened to her, took care of her, and finally, she moved into his apartment. It was the beginning of the love of a lifetime." Terry looked up. His eyes bore the sadness of someone driven too far to find happiness ever again. "Imagine her . . . bottomless grief when my father died in an accident." He bit his lower lip, but the tears came, nevertheless. "I rushed to her. I was with her whenever possible, but — " He broke off, hanging his head.

"It's all right," Matthew said quietly. "We understand how you must've felt."

"Whatever I did it wasn't enough. *I* wasn't enough. Without Jim, she didn't want to live anymore." Terry ran a hand through his hair, then emptied the glass. He didn't bother to wipe away his tears. "When I came in and found her . . . bleeding in the bathtub, it was too late to save her. I blame myself for not being the son she needed."

"We understand your grief, Mr. Winters. Nevertheless, we need to clear up the circumstances. Four of the five women of the former high school clique are dead." Matthew watched Terry's eyes widen, and he appeared to stop breathing. "And Carla Demasio is the fifth woman of that clique, and still missing."

"You're saying . . ." Words failed him. Terry's face lost all color as he stared at Matthew. His lips parted, but he needed time to find his voice. He stuttered. "You're saying, not only my mom is dead, but four women of the group she was friends with at high school?"

"They had moved, changed names due to marriages, and yet the killer found them." Matthew cocked his head. "All of that happened after the death of your mother."

"Oh, my god." Terry had trouble breathing. His hands shook. "You mean these poor women were killed *because* my mother committed suicide? That's insane."

"We haven't obtained tangible evidence so far, but there is

a correlation between your mother's suicide and the ensuing kidnappings and murders. Do you want to tell us anything about it?"

"What should I tell you? Until now, I had no idea about these murders, and now you think there's a connection between my mom and those other women?" He shook his head, looking ill. He gestured with his right hand. "But the women and that clique—that was more than thirty-five years ago! Why do you think—"

"For one, they knew each other."

"And I think you've known about that for a long time," Jason said in his no-nonsense voice.

Terry got up to stand behind the couch as if trying to bring distance between Jason and himself. His loud breathing filled the room. "I know about it? What should I know?" His ignorance sounded hollow.

"You had several old pictures—probably from your mother's youth, on your cell phone. I pulled the yearbooks and found one match."

"Yes, I had—"

"Why did you put these pictures on your phone?"

Matthew glanced at his partner and shook his head slightly.

"I just wanted to have them with me," Terry said, holding tight to the backrest. He looked alarmed, and his breath came in fits and starts. "A memory . . . of a life lost. Do you want to use this against me?"

"You've given us a lot of nonsense so far, Mr. Winters." Jason folded his hands and bent forward, keeping Terry in his stare. "First, you claim you ran because you were a shoplifter once. Then, you claim that I resembled a father from the kindergarten and that you and your partner wouldn't want to be seen together. Now I want to know why you keep these pictures on your phone—not the wedding photo of your parents, which would be a logical choice — but five pictures from Margie Winters's high school time. Snapshots with her friends. Explain that to me. And while you're at it, tell me who you met this morning in an alley, six miles away from the kindergarten."

Terry paled even more, and sweat beaded his brow. "You were observing me?"

"Obviously." Jason opened and closed his folded hands. "Please, we're listening."

When Terry ran a hand through his hair this time, the strands stuck on his head, damp with sweat. He looked around, but without his partner he had no one to turn to, no one who helped him out of the situation. He breathed in and out, then hung his head again. For a moment, he appeared to lose control completely.

Matthew wondered whether Jason had been right all along, and the friendly face was nothing but a façade for a man with many skeletons in his closet.

"Sit down!" Jason ordered.

Terry's eyes widened as if Jason had threatened him with bodily harm. Matthew was tense as a bowstring, ready to jump should the suspect decide to run. It wouldn't be a clever move to escape, but in many cases despair forced a man to do stupid actions.

Slowly, looking haunted and afraid, Terry sat down again. He reached for the bottle at the side of the table and poured a drink, hardly able to fill the glass. His gaze flickered from Jason to Matthew and back. "It's not how you think it is."

Matthew shrugged and let his honey-smooth voice work for him. "Then tell us how it is."

Terry appeared to shrink on the couch. "After my mom's death, a lawyer called me and told me that someone tried to contact me. The lawyer explained that my mom had left a letter at his office, only to be opened after her death. It was meant for someone called Timothy Ellwood." He gulped the alcohol and put down the empty glass.

Jason pulled his notebook and pen. "Timothy Ellwood. He's a relative?"

"My half-brother. *Ellwood* was my mother's maiden name."

"The name of the lawyer?" Jason asked, pen poised.

"I can't recall. I'm . . . I'm . . ." He pulled at the hem of his thin pullover. The trembling got worse, and more tears trickled down his cheeks. "I'd have to look it up."

"Fine. Keep that in mind."

"Did you make contact with your half-brother?" Matthew wanted to know.

"I did. Imagine my surprise." He pulled up his nose. "I hadn't known I had a brother. Mom had never mentioned him, and I wondered why. I took the number and called Timothy. When I met with him for the first time in a restaurant, he was exuberant to have a brother — someone who could tell him about the mother he hadn't come to know." Terry paused to breathe deeply, obviously trying to find words to sum up the feelings his half-brother had evoked. "He was born when she was nineteen, five months after the car accident." Terry looked up. The pain in his eyes was raw. "She had seen no other option but to give him up for adoption."

Nicolas's shoulders were agony now that the straps of the backpack pressed into his muscles constantly. The ensuing pain where the bullet had nicked him was worsening his condition. Nick remembered an old case, in which he had pursued a killer through woodland — wounded, exhausted, close to collapsing. He had not given up, and he would fight harder this time knowing that Jacklyn's life depended on him. He led the way and turned around frequently to see whether she was coming or if she needed help.

Jacklyn told him she was fine, but he knew better. Never before in her life had she been forced to run through unknown territory, hunted by a lunatic who wanted them both dead. He couldn't imagine her condition, only heard her strained breathing. She tried to keep up with him, and he gave her credit for not collapsing on one of the rock formations and calling it a day.

"I need . . . to look at the wound," she said, breathless. "Please, I don't . . ."

He stopped and turned around. "Do you need a break?"

"That, too." Jacklyn was sweating profusely, and her hair clung to her face. "I know you want to run, but —"

"No, it's okay. Let's take a few minutes." He took off the backpack and handed her a water bottle. "We don't know for how long we'll be here, so —"

"I get it. Just a mouthful." She exhaled. The fine lines around her eyes and nose were deeper, and her expression told of unspoken worry. Though she tried to cloak it, the deep-set eyes revealed her exhaustion. She handed him the bottle. "You, too. And let me see the wound."

"You won't give up, huh?" Nicolas sat beside her and peeled off his long jacket. The movement sent painful stings up to his neck. "It's just a small —"

"It's a wound, and wounds tend to get infected." Jacklyn cut half the sleeve of the pullover to have a look. "There's dirt and fibers in it. I didn't find any disinfectant in their bathroom, so a dressing must do for now. If we find another creek, I'll wash it, but I won't put my dirty fingers in there."

"It won't get infected. Remember, I'm one of the resilient guys. They don't suffer from such minor injuries." Nicolas made a face to trigger a smile but failed. Her mouth twitched, and he realized she was too scared of both the killer and him falling sick. "Listen, Jacky, I mean it. It's highly unusual that such a —"

"It was an old gun, an old bullet with rust on it, I bet." She worked with the dressing, and the simple activity appeared to calm her. "Do you think your body knows how to fight this?"

"Yes, I think so." He watched her fasten the dressing with steady hands. "Thanks. That'll do. Ready to go on?"

Jacklyn stowed the rest of the rudimental first aid kit in the backpack and got up. "Yep."

Nicolas put on his long jacket and the backpack and fought not to hiss with pain but keep a stoic expression that would give her courage. He wouldn't fail her.

He must not fail her.

After his mother's violent death, Keith had fallen into a kind of trance. It was a state of mind like a bubble aside from reality that neither Aunt Ronnie nor Uncle Joe could penetrate. He ate, he slept, he even washed himself once a week, but he was only functioning in a rudimental way. For four weeks, he denied the possibility that his mother was dead, killed by some lunatic the police didn't catch. An officer from the Portland homicide division talked with him, asked silly questions about enemies of the family and whether Keith knew of anyone bearing a grudge against her. He even asked whether Jeffrey might have returned and taken revenge on his wife. Keith didn't recall having answered any questions, but he remembered Ronnie's voice in the background, a soothing murmur. Her hand touched his hair as if were ten years old again and needed to be calmed.

He didn't want consolation. He wanted his mother back, the one person he relied on, the one person he needed to make his life worth living. She was his partner, even more so after the death of his father. But she remained in heaven, as Ronnie told him whenever he asked. She said that Shelley's life might have been much brighter if she had a nice, good-looking husband with a brain and money, something so many rich hikers from the cities had — those arrogant intruders, who claimed they needed some time off from their stressful lives by hiking through the woods and thus chasing away the game. Aunt Ronnie claimed she knew that happiness was based on a strong husband and money — that applied to every couple in every situation. Her sister had had bad luck meeting someone like Jeffrey, who was the greatest loser ever walking God's sacred earth.

Keith realized that it was his task — and his mother's voice in his head confirmed that — to bring all those arrogant and ignorant couples who drove cross-country with their expensive SUVs to justice. He had to confront them with their fears and show them that they were unfit to survive.

The old van suffered more cutouts than before but made it to Uncle Joe's cabin, rattling as if it would fall apart any second. Keith ran toward the door, expecting to find his aunt and uncle keeping the intruders in check. When he opened the door, he stopped, shocked to the core.

He didn't see any intruder — just his poor aunt and her husband on the floor, bound and helpless. Uncle Joe had an ugly dark red bruise on his left cheek, and his aunt's eyes were red from weeping. Keith felt such rage flood his system that his face flushed, and when he wanted to ask a question, he couldn't do more than produce guttural sounds in his throat.

"Finally!" Joe shouted. "Untie us! Quick!"

Joe's voice shook Keith out of his state of shock, and he hurried toward his uncle, freed him and Aunt Ronnie, and listened to their story of the Hayes terrorizing them in the most brutal way.

"They ran off about three hours ago," Aunt Ronnie said. "Where were you, Keith? I expected you much sooner."

Keith blushed, aware that his indecision had taken more time than he thought. "I brought the spare tires," he said instead of an excuse. "I can mount them if you want me to."

"No! Keith, we want you to follow the couple. They hurt us, and I don't want them to get away with it — not like all the other rich scumbags who think they own the woods."

Aunt Ronnie looked Keith deep in the eyes, a gesture that never failed its purpose. Keith nodded in immediate compliance.

"You have to find them and bring them to justice," Uncle Joe stated in his deep voice. "We can call the sheriff and tell them that you'll bring him two robbers who claim they were kidnapped." Joe lowered his wobbling chin and pursed his lips. "Nonsense, right?"

Keith nodded emphatically. "Nonsense."

"Good boy." Joe slapped Keith's shoulder, and his worry dissolved in a smile. "Now, off you go and do what we couldn't. Don't let them escape."

Keith helped his uncle get up and led him to a chair. "Where did they go?"

"Not along the path." Aunt Ronnie made it to her feet and drank tea from a cup. "They would not want to meet you. So my best guess is they're turning south to find the road." She pierced Keith with her glare, and he knew this task ahead was important. "They broke in, used our stuff, ate what we had stored, and then, when we figured out their scheme, knocked us out and left us here — tied up! If you hadn't come, we would have died here!"

"Now, now," Joe said, chuckling. "They knew Keith would show up, right?"

Keith had trouble concentrating on the conversation. He wanted to run, not to listen. "Three hours ago, southern direction. Did they take anything with them?"

"Yes, water and food, and some dressings from the bath-room. Joe shot the man," she said proudly.

"So he will be slow?"

"Not really." Joe winked at Keith as he helped himself to a glass of bourbon, his only guilty pleasure, as he claimed. "The old gun almost ripped my arm off. At best it's a flesh wound, not much harm done."

"What a pity." Aunt Ronnie growled. "But she's weaker than him. She'll slow him down."

"Fine." Keith stood and almost made it to the door when his aunt caught up with him for a goodbye kiss.

"Do justice," she said, as if tasking him with changing the tires.

He understood what she meant. He shouldered his back-pack, grabbed the rifle, and set out, looking for footprints.

CHAPTER TEN

Terry needed more alcohol before he could continue, but his hands were still shaking.

To expedite the proceedings, Matthew poured for him. "Tell us about Timothy, please."

"We phoned, and he wanted to meet me, as soon as possible. I thought it would be great to have someone . . . to talk to." Terry held tight to the small glass and didn't meet Matthew's gaze. "When I couldn't fathom what had happened to me—I was an orphan suddenly and my world turned upside down—he appeared like a light in the darkness. Someone I could talk to about my mom and dad. Aside from Harold, I mean." He looked up, pleadingly. "I met with him, and we talked for hours—virtually until the waiter asked us to leave because they were closing." A smile came and went. "Tim—the *Bear* as he wanted to be called—wanted to know everything about mom. What she liked and disliked, what she achieved, and what kind of person my dad had been. Everything about the family, you know."

"What did he tell you about himself?" Jason asked, which shook Terry out of his contemplation.

"He's named the *Bear* for a reason—he's tall and broad, so unlike me in any way. Guess there's truth to the genetic code—that the boys inherit mostly from their fathers. I admit I was . . . intimidated by his . . . strength and bearing." Quietly, he said, "I didn't ask many questions." When Jason raised his brows in disbelief, Terry dropped his gaze at the glass in his hand. "But he was friendly, kind, and very generous. He insisted on paying for dinner."

"How did he grow up? Did he bear a grudge that your mother didn't raise him like she raised you?"

"I can't tell. From what he told me, he lived in a foster home, but was adopted when he was six months old, so he didn't know of his adoption at all. His parents left him in the dark. He was an adult when he found out the truth."

"Did he say he was shocked or angry about that?"

Matthew held his breath. He knew where the conversation was going, and Terry didn't look like he wanted to incriminate his half-brother.

"No, just surprised and, I think, disappointed." Terry shrugged. "Think of it—you learn you're adopted, and you try to find out about your biological parents." He paused to look around the room. "But he didn't find out anything until he received the formal letter from my—*our*—mother's lawyer and that was after her death."

The bitterness in Terry's voice alarmed Matthew. He sensed that the younger brother envied the elder one for a letter he had been denied.

"Do you know its contents?"

"Tim told me mom had written an apology, telling him that she saw no other option at that time—she had been alone and unable to take care of a child. It seemed the best option for her, and Tim said he didn't blame her. That's why he wanted to know all about the years after the accident and his birth. He tried to understand the circumstances of her life, and I told him the stories she had told me." Terry appeared to get a grip on his emotions again. He put down the glass. "Tim said his parents weren't a model for loving couples. Though his home was okay, money was tight, and they quarreled a lot. When I heard that, I kept back that my mom and dad were the happiest couple on earth. I can't recall a day they were arguing.

They had different opinions, but that was about it."

He took a deep breath, then got up again. "Tim . . . wished he had known her. He wanted to collect every little thing about her — that's why I showed him the high school pictures. In a later meeting, Tim dropped the line that he would be happy to talk with other people who had known her and could tell him about her character and what she did back then." He wiped his hands along his sweat pants again.

"Do you think he tried to spot the high school girlfriends?"

Terry ran a hand through his hair, made a face, and hesitated to answer. "You must understand how he felt. He had been denied his true relatives — his mother and whoever his father may be — all of his life. So when he gets the answer, she's already dead, and he's got no chance to talk to her. He wants to . . . picture her, form an image in his mind. He wants to know all about her — whatever it might be. So, yes, I think he might have tried to locate mom's old friends." He shrugged and stared at the floor again. His voice was quiet and cautious. "Maybe he contacted the high school in Portland."

"Did he say anything about his biological father? Did your mother mention him in the letter?"

"He didn't say so. He said it was a short letter, hand-written. She encouraged him to contact his half-brother."

Matthew pondered whether Terry or Timothy was telling the truth. "Did he ever mention his real name?"

"Real name? What do you mean?"

"You said he was adopted, which means he can't have your mother's maiden name *Ellwood,* but that of his adoptive parents."

"That's . . . right." Terry frowned, and suddenly a violent shiver ran through him. "No, he said his name was Timothy Ellwood. He never used another name, and I admit I didn't check the name on his credit card. I had no doubt that my mother might have left the name with him. Or wanted him to use it. I don't know."

"Do you know where he works?"

"No." He shook his head, frowning. He chose his words cautiously. "He never mentioned a profession. That's odd, because he wanted to know what I do right away. But now that you mention it—he never told me about his occupation—if he had one. He seemed to have plenty of time."

"But you said he had money."

"Yes, he always paid for the drinks and meals." Terry's face regained a healthier color, mostly because of the amount of alcohol he had been drinking.

"Did he tell you about any journeys or about his search for old friends of your mother?"

"No. We met several times, and it was always pleasant— friendly. He seemed to enjoy his life, in spite of the not-so-loving parents. Tim said he looked forward, and that he was glad he had met with me. We could stay in contact, reminisce about mom, and support each other." Terry's smile was short-lived. "It sounded good to me."

"Do you know where he lives? His address?"

"I never asked. He didn't visit me here, either, because I wanted to keep Harold out of this reunion. We met in pubs and diners, in public places."

"The way you say it, you haven't seen him recently. Did you lose contact?"

"Tim didn't say a word the last time he was here—"

"When was that?"

"About three weeks ago."

"Since then you've had no contact? No calls?"

"No."

"And with whom did you meet this morning?" Jason asked. "Was that him?"

Terry looked like he'd been hit by a whip. "I already told

you, it had nothing to do with Tim."

"Then tell us what this meeting was about." Jason stared at him, relentless. "Who did you meet and what did you do?"

"I'm planning Harold's birthday party." Terry's gaze switched to the table again. Though he'd had quite a bit to drink, he appeared tense and uneasy. "We've been together for two years by now, and I want to surprise him with something special."

"Drugs?"

"No!" Terry lifted his hands in defense, and once more his eyes were wide. "We'd never use drugs! How dare you assume—"

"Then what was this meeting about?"

Terry wet his lips, avoiding Jason's glare. "Harold's the one who makes most of the money. He pays for both rents and for everything else we need. I earn much less, and I had to pay for two funerals and the household liquidation. I'm still recovering financially. But Harold's cell phone is very old. He's not one to look after such things, but the new phones can do so much more. I wanted to buy him a new one." He looked up, defiantly. "I tried to get one on the street."

"From a fence."

"Yes."

"You know that it's illegal?"

"Yes." He got up and showed Jason the box with the brand-new cell phone. "Will that do?"

Matthew exchanged glances with Jason before he went on. "What else did you learn about Timothy?"

"Not much." Terry put the box on the table. "He appeared to be a man used to making his own decisions. A man with a clear view of the world. I admit we didn't talk about world politics but mostly about my mom and how her life had been. Then he asked about me. He wanted to know what I was doing for a living, and I told him anecdotes of my work at the kindergarten. He seemed to love that." A smile came and went. "Children can be fun."

"Did you reveal your kind of relationship?"

"I'm careful with that. No, I didn't tell him about Harold or how I live."

"We need you to come to the office again and sit with an artist. We need a sketch of Timothy."

Terry flinched as he got up. "You think he's got something to do with the murders?"

"At the very least, we would like to talk with him about his time abroad." Jason stood. "You should've come forward with the story about your half-brother right away, Mr. Winters. Lying to the FBI is a federal crime."

"I didn't lie."

Matthew stopped Jason's lecturing with a warning glance before he turned back to Terry. "Find the name and address of the lawyer. We also expect you to accompany us to the FBI right away."

Jason straightened to his full height. "If you don't cooperate—"

"I get it." Terry pressed his lips tight. "You're accusing me of all the things you just listed so you can arrest me and drag me away in handcuffs again."

Jason smiled. "That sums it up quite nicely."

"I want us to take dancing lessons," Jacklyn said as they were making good progress through a less dense part of the woods, still following an unseen trail that would take them to a road, hopefully.

Nicolas glanced at her over his shoulder. "Dancing lessons? Why on earth should I take dancing lessons?"

"My parents will celebrate their fortieth anniversary next year. It'll be a huge ball at their home, and I would like to dance with you. It would be fun."

Nicolas heard the silent accusation about his meager interest, but he couldn't bring himself to show eagerness when his thoughts circled around *how* and *when* they would leave these damned woods behind them.

"I don't have time for this, Jacky. You know my working schedule. When there's a case, I can't drop everything to rush to a dancing lesson."

"We would take private lessons we could schedule whenever you have time."

"And I can't promise to be there. Yes, I do understand you're interested in having a mutual hobby," he said, interrupting her plea. "But it doesn't fit with my irregular duties. When I'm on a case, I might come home late at night. You know that."

"It's wrong not to try." Jacklyn slipped on a mossy patch and caught herself before he could. "You're always working. I know that you don't have an office job where you can put down your pen and leave. Is that everything you want?"

"Please, don't make this an argument about my job again. I would like to do so many things with you, and you know that, but I think it's wrong to start something new and then cancel every second lesson because I'm out of town for an investigation."

Her silence was an even stronger accusation than her words. He stopped and turned to her. "Jacky, please, I try not to work too much overtime. I do this for you even though it leads to quarrels with my boss now and then. I want us to spend time together. Taking up another obligation — like weekly dancing lessons — is just — "

"You're saying you've got unpredictable working hours. All right. But does that mean we can't do anything together aside from some running late in the evening?"

Nicolas knew her well enough. She wouldn't budge. She

would get what she wanted. Not right away, but with her constant nagging she would bring him to the point where he couldn't deny her wish anymore. She was invincible when it came to perseverance.

"Jacky, it's—"

"Think about it," she said and walked on. "Think about the priorities in your life and what you expect to have in five or ten years."

It was a hard slap, and Nicolas had no means to counter it. He overtook her on the slope and walked more carefully when the hillside got steeper. Half a mile south, their path filled with so many rocks that he stopped to assess the easiest route.

"We have to move more slowly now," he said, keeping his voice down to business. "I walk first, and you follow my steps. If I slip, wait and search for another way. All right?"

Jacklyn didn't reply, but her look said he shouldn't get too cocky. Nicolas understood he was walking on treacherous grounds—both literally and figuratively. He concentrated on the rocks at his feet. It was much easier than musing how he might dodge the dancing lesson obligation. He liked music, but he had never been a dancer. He felt clumsy and much too tall when leading a woman on the dancefloor. He had tried it in his adolescence and found out that any other sport was easier to manage than moving gracefully on slippery parquet.

Nicolas heard Jacklyn's boot kick loose some small stones, and before he could turn and lend her a hand, she slipped on the edge, lost hold with her hands, and fell onto his back, crying out. He had no time to brace for the impact, could only resist her weight to soften her fall, and yet, when he thought the moment over, he became aware he was standing on a grassy knob that didn't hold his weight. In a split second, he was bound to fall. He turned around to grab Jacklyn and pull her to the side so that they landed on soil instead of sharp rocks. However, the impact knocked all air out of his lungs. Jacklyn screamed as they tumbled downslope. He tried to keep her close to his body, but then he hit another obstacle, and she rolled away from him while he was stuck against a tree stump.

As fast as he could, Nicolas got back on his feet and hastened to catch up with Jacklyn. She lay fifteen feet away, closer to the rocks. "Jacky!" She didn't move. Nicolas slipped the remaining distance on his feet and butt and stopped beside her. "Jacky, hey, are you all right?"

Her eyes remained closed, and she gave no sign that she could hear him. Carefully, he pulled her limp body in his arms. He remained clear-headed in a shootout, but seeing Jacklyn on the wet soil, unmoving, blew away his equanimity. He panicked that she wouldn't wake up again. "No, Jacky, don't do this to me."

Back at the office, Matthew and Jason found a note from the agent in charge of the HRT, Donovan Nichols. Jason shook his head and went straight for the cafeteria, so it was up to Matthew to make the call.

"This is Agent Montagna. What's the news?"

"I'm afraid it's bad news," Agent Nichols said and sighed. "While we waited for the kidnapper to make contact, Washington PD called us. A passerby found a badly wounded woman matching Carla Demasio's description in an alley in Arlington. The man reported to the EMS that she whispered a name—*Clifford Hazelton*—before she passed out."

"What kind of injuries did she suffer?" Matthew took down the name.

"Multiple knife wounds to her face and torso—liver and stomach perforated. The doctors give her a ten percent chance of survival. It doesn't look good."

"So it's fair to assume it was the same killer that murdered the other women?"

"I'm not that much into the case, but—yes, I'd say you're dealing with the *Mutilator*. I'll pull traffic camera footage and call in CSU. Right now, we're asking around the block whether anyone has seen a vehicle parked in the alley."

"Send me the file, please, and the information about the hospital and the doctor who's treating her."

"Will do."

Matthew put down the receiver, wrote down the details, and pinned the piece of paper on the whiteboard Jason used for the collection of crime details. After Matthew's break-through, Jason had dutifully listed all evidence and connections between the persons. Matthew wished that the homicide division of the Portland PD had noticed earlier that they were dealing with a serial killer. Yet, as he stared at the notes, Matthew had the gut feeling that the series might stop now — the five women of the high school clique were dead, or respectively close to dying.

After another excellent cup of coffee and with Jason still indulging in his lunch, Matthew put a question mark behind Margie Winters and her two sons. He added the questions,

What did Margie write in the letter to Timothy? What's his real name?

Did Margie reveal the biological father's name?

What did Timothy share with Terry, and did Terry tell us the truth about the revelations?

Does Terry support Timothy in any other way than sharing memories?

Did Timothy threaten Terry to help him (Terry intimidated by Timothy)

Who is Clifford Hazelton?

A quick search on the internet revealed three Clifford Hazeltons. One of them had been a rich British banker in Portland but was retired now. He had made a lot of money buying and selling real estate forty years ago and was a local celebrity in the Portland, Maine, area. He had four kids from three marriages. Pictures showed him with his recent lover, a woman at least thirty years younger and very pretty. He used to spend his time on golf courses. He also sponsored young talents, both in golf and tennis, and attended competitions throughout the year. The media considered him a bon vivant, and Matthew could only confirm that impression. Hazelton looked much younger than his years and like a man who took every challenge to get under a woman's skirt. The latest flame would not be the last one.

There was no information about Hazelton's residence or how to contact the owner. Matthew found an email and a phone number of his assistant, though. He printed the information and put it on the whiteboard.

He called the assistant, Mr. Donovan Adley, after lunchtime, explained the circumstances of his interest in Mr. Hazelton, and hoped for a clue to the connection between Mrs. Demasio and Mr. Hazelton.

"Mr. Hazelton is out of town," Mr. Adley said in a typical British accent. "He's not expected to return prior to May eighth. I don't see any need to bother Mr. Hazelton with your request, Agent Montagna. Who can tell what this woman said, close to dying, as you pointed out? There are quite a few men by the name of Hazelton. What makes you so sure that my employer is the one you need to talk to?"

"First, he has spent most of his life in Portland, Maine, which fits the circumstances I'm dealing with in this case. Second, there are only three men by that name, not a hundred. The other two live far away from Portland."

Mr. Adley scoffed. "Still I don't see any reason to interrupt

Mr. Hazelton's vacation. I'll take down a note to discuss the matter with him upon his return."

Matthew was losing his good mood. He was about to ask why a retiree needed a vacation. "You're dealing with the FBI, Mr. Adley. Obstructing my investigation is a federal crime. I want his number and his whereabouts. Right now. It's possible that a serial killer has him on his list."

"I tried to reach him this morning, but he didn't take the call." Mr. Adley sounded miffed. "Currently, I don't know where he is. He should be at the golf course close to Bangor, but the manager told me he left yesterday. Should I reach him, I'll certainly tell him about the threat."

"Do that. Fax me all locations where he might be and add the telephone numbers." After he ended the call, Matthew leaned back in his chair, his good mood blown away. "Maybe Mr. Adley needs to see the knife of the killer come his way to be more cooperative," Matthew mumbled into his beard.

Jason looked stuffed when he sat down, smiling. "You're gonna kill someone? Well, what a pity I wasn't here." He patted his sizeable paunch. "Lunch was good today. You should've come."

Matthew brought him up to speed. "Any ideas about Mr. Hazelton?"

"The young women originated in Portland and the surrounding towns. We should dig into their environment again. Maybe Mr. Hazelton had a connection with them — via tennis or golf, who knows?"

"Always a bon vivant? Why not?" Matthew sighed. "Though I don't like it, I'm going to inform our Portland field office that they'd better keep an eye on Mr. Hazelton in case someone with a pointy knife shows up."

CHAPTER ELEVEN

Carefully, Nicolas pulled Jacklyn in his arms to palpate the back of her head for injuries. He sighed with relief when he didn't find any blood. "Hey, my love, come back to me. Please, wake up."

In his training, he had learned to stay calm and vigilant and not to draw rash conclusions. Seeing Jacklyn unresponsive, Nicolas had to force his breathing down to think clearly. She didn't appear to have broken any bones, and there was no open wound he had to treat. There was a chance that she had only hit her head, but his heart was racing, and his mind flooded with dreadful images.

He looked downslope. There were at least two more miles of rocks, slippery grass, and dense wood to cover. If he had to carry Jacklyn, he would be much slower, and there was a good chance that the killer would catch up with them before nightfall.

He touched her cool face and kissed her lips as if the action would wake her up like *Sleeping Beauty*. A bruise showed on her right temple. The thought of a concussion came and went. He wouldn't know about her condition if she didn't wake up and talk to him. However, they needed to get away as quickly as possible. The killer could take position at the top of the hill and aim without being in danger of Nicolas. The image of losing Jacklyn while they were close to safety turned his panic into the need for action. He wouldn't wait.

While he prepared for departure, she made a sound in her throat, and he bent over her. "Hey, are you with me?"

"Are we there yet?" she whispered.

"Getting closer." He smiled when she opened her eyes. "How are you feeling?"

"Like I hit a kettledrum." She sat up with his help.

"Any double vision?"

"Can't tell." Jacklyn held her head and sobbed. "I want to go home, Nick. Please. I don't know how long I can keep this up. I know you're doing what you can, but—I'm not *Lara Croft*. I can pretend for some time, but this—this is too much for me." She looked up with tears in her eyes.

Her misery tore at his heart. "I know." He knelt beside her, gazing uphill. "I wish I could speed this up, but—"

"You can't." She wiped her eyes and made it to her feet. He held her hands when she swayed. "Okay. I'm okay. You know that I'll walk on until I collapse. I don't want to be shot or see you die." She looked around, hopeless, exhausted, and in pain. "This is so big. I feel trapped in some giant game and don't know how to find the exit."

He kissed her brow. Her worries were his own, and seeing her so downbeat hurt him bodily. "Listen, it can't be much farther. We'll find the road and stop someone."

"I so want to believe you." She took a deep breath and straightened. With a fake smile she said, "Let's go."

He steadied her when she stumbled. "Watch your step."

"Don't be so damn . . . helpful."

Nicolas held her in his arms. "I'll do everything for you, and if you can't walk I'll carry you."

"No, no, that's going too far. I'm not seriously injured. I'll walk."

"Jacky—"

"Don't say it. Maybe you cloak it better than I do, but you're tired, too."

"You're right." They walked on. "The killer knows the woods much better, like his home. He could be anywhere—

even overtaking us and waiting at a perfect hideout." He looked over his shoulder. He couldn't forget her limp body and the minutes he had feared she wouldn't wake up.

"That's not helpful." Jacklyn tripped again, bit her lips not to cry out, and scoffed. "I'm thirty-eight, and I'm not made for this. I don't have a job with a sports program and weekly combat training. I'm . . ." She broke off.

"I understand."

"Do you?"

Nicolas had no idea what he could do aside from lending her a hand or taking her in his arms. "It's not that bad right now. We have water, we have food, and the weather's dry. I'm sure I'm keeping one direction, which means that we're gonna hit a road sooner than later."

"Is that so?"

"It's a logical assumption." He did everything to sound optimistic. "Without marks along the route, most hikers run in circles."

"What's this over there — to the left? Are those shoes? And a chain?"

Nicolas followed her hint and stopped dead in his tracks so that she caught up with him.

"Please, don't let us find a body here. I couldn't stomach that. It's too much."

"Stay here. I'll have a look."

"But —"

"If he's dead, you'd better not get close. You don't need to see this. Okay? Wait here."

During the afternoon, Matthew realized that no one was better than Jason Beckham when it came to dissecting a case. He took down notes, created a timeline, and added important details highlighted in yellow or orange. In addition, he displayed pictures and maps of the crime scenes with dates and evidence.

Matthew sat on the edge of the table, astonished at Jason's masterpiece.

"We also know what Timothy looks like," Jason said pointing at the sketch. "And we have the name of the lawyer. I spoke with a judge. He'll authorize us to ask for the recipient's name and address. We'll have the court order by tomorrow morning."

"I handed the copies to the media division. Every police station and the papers will have them in an hour. The search warrant is printed as we speak." He frowned. "I might see what I want to see, but do you think Timothy Ellwood resembles Clifford Hazelton?"

"Not much. He's tall and broad, but that's about it." Jason swung back on his chair. "The lawyer, Mr. Scott Gilford, has scheduled us for eight o'clock in the morning. He didn't want to reveal anything about Timothy on the phone, and I hope he won't cause too much trouble. Client's privileges etcetera. Can you make it?"

"Sure. Can I bring Bingo? He's a great guy."

"You're kidding me. You won't bring your dog!" Jason turned back to his computer screen. "Summing up — Clifford Hazelton was one of many rich men at the Portland golf club back in the days. He was a known charmer — as there were many others — and he was a generous man."

Matthew laughed. "With both his money and his semen." He laughed harder upon seeing Jason's sour expression.

"Moving on. Rumor has it that Mr. Hazelton and several other club members employed young women at the bar and as caddies. They were paid for entertaining the men, which might or might not have led to private hours in private rooms. The information here is sketchy at best."

Matthew nodded. "These exclusive clubs are like the old men's clubs in Great Britain. Whatever happens there, no one talks about, not even former employees."

"Looking at the family history of the young women, we find out that Amber Fowler and Madeleine Green gave birth to children when they were eighteen and nineteen years old, respectively."

"Which fits with Margie Winters's — or at that time Margie *Ellwood's* — pregnancy. Interesting." Matthew sat up straight. "Are you suggesting the rich men got the women pregnant?"

"In both cases, the fathers were not named on the birth certificates. The mothers simply didn't reveal the names, and that's it. But it fits with them working at the club. Obviously, they didn't know about birth control at that time or didn't think about it." Jason pointed at yet another piece of evidence. "We also know that Carla Demasio was unable to have children after an abortion went wrong —"

"Let me guess — while she was nineteen years old?"

"Twenty, but you get the brownie point. All of this — and knowing about Margie Winters' pregnancy — leads to the conclusion that her first-born son is our prime suspect for murder."

Nicolas took a deep breath as he moved toward the large pine tree. He saw a thick chain around the trunk and the legs of a person, possible male, in black jeans and hiking boots. He wore a thick silver manacle around his left ankle and did not move.

He heard Jacklyn sit on the ground. She leaned against a trunk, sighing with relief for the brief pause. He wouldn't be surprised to find her dozing upon his return.

Nicolas looked uphill once more, afraid the killer was closing in. They had lost time due to the tricky path and Jacklyn's unconsciousness. It wouldn't be until they were in trouble. So far, Nicolas had no idea how to counter the maniac's precision with the rifle. He didn't intend to wait and find out how good the stranger truly was.

Nicolas rounded the tree to have a closer look. The man wore a thick pullover and an expensive black parka. The way he was dressed, he was one of those hikers Veronica had talked about—a rich guy from the city, on tour in Maine's woods. But he was dirty, from his dark blond hair over his clothes down to his boots. He reeked of sweat and excrement, and the soil around the tree was churned up as if he had walked in circles many times. A small empty water bottle lay beside him.

"Sir? All you all right?"

The stranger stirred, then made a sound in his throat. When he looked up, his eyes were wild, his moves erratic. Expelling his breath, he lifted his hands as if to ward off an attack and moved backward, against the trunk. Nicolas could tell by his deranged appearance that he had been here for days. He was shivering badly. Nicolas considered it a miracle that he was still responsive. He appeared to have more stamina than met the eye. However, his lips were parched, and he couldn't form words.

Nicolas unpacked a water bottle and held it to his lips.

"Drink slowly. Small sips," he warned when the man tried to snap the bottle from his hands. He signaled Jacklyn thumbs up. She got up and joined them. "Can you tell us your name?"

"Da . . . David." He held tight to the water bottle, and though he followed the advice, he coughed and grimaced when the cold water reached his stomach. "David Callahan."

"I'm Nick, and this is my fiancé, Jacky."

"Who did this to you?" Jacklyn asked, horrified.

"The killer who kidnaps the couples." David coughed again. Nicolas helped him sit up. "He left me here, and I don't know where he took Rebecca."

"She's your wife?"

"My girlfriend." David grabbed Nicolas's arm. His blue eyes were wide and terrified. "Can you free me? Please, I've been here so long. I . . . I tried everything, but the chain's too thick. I couldn't break it. Don't let me die here."

"I'll see what I can do." Nicolas felt uneasy losing more time, but it was out of question to leave the man behind. He looked at the cuff around David's ankle and shook his head. "That's a new lock. I can't open it."

"Oh, my god, please, you must do something!" He thanked Jacklyn for the cookies she handed him with the distinct warning to eat slowly.

"I'll try the padlock. That's old. I guess I can do that."

David gave him room, ate the cookies, and wanted more. While he gobbled a small piece of cheese, Nicolas inserted the pointed knife between the body and shackle of the lock, listening to the sound of the metal.

"For how long have you been here?" Jacklyn asked, her voice full of sympathy.

"Three days." David shivered so violently that his words came out in incoherent intervals. "The bastard took my girlfriend away and then dragged me here. I think . . . I think he murdered her and buried her somewhere."

"I'm sorry."

"How did you get here? Were you hiking?"

"The killer is after us, too."

"He is?" David shouted. He was on his feet and stepped backward until the chain went taut. "Oh, god, no! You have to hurry! We must get away! Right now! He'll kill us all!"

Nicolas looked up. "I'm trying. Just don't move until I get this, all right?"

David wiped his dirty face, drank more water, and watched Nicolas with feverish urgency. "He's a monster. He had us locked up in a hole in the ground, and then he took Rebecca away. We quarreled. I didn't mean to, but—then he dragged me here and left me to die." He paused, sobbing. "I just wanted to write a story. I didn't mean to—"

"You're a reporter?" Jacklyn asked.

"Yes, *Bangor Gazette*. I wrote the first article about the couple killer."

Nicolas scoffed. "Now I know why your name is familiar. You also wrote about the Portland citizen who had been wrongfully imprisoned."

"That's right. Police and FBI messed this up big time." David got up and stared uphill. He wiped his mouth. "Did you see him?"

"The *couple killer*?" Jacklyn sounded incredulous. "So he did this before?"

"Yes, several times. He attacks rich couples on side roads and kidnaps them. None of them were ever found. Police and the FBI are completely in the dark. Again. Or should I say *still*?"

Jacklyn paled and held a hand across her mouth. "How many?"

"Seven couples. Fourteen people. Then came Rebecca and me." David grabbed Nicolas's shoulder. His eyes were wide, his voice loud. "Please, can't you do that faster? We need to get away from here!"

"Stop it!" Jacklyn ordered. "He's doing what he can, okay? Stop pestering him."

"But if the killer is on his way—"

"We're in danger, too."

"But you haven't been shackled to a tree *for three days*! I'll lose my mind if I don't get away from here!"

Nicolas didn't hear the lock snap open because the same moment, Jacklyn slapped David's face. "Get a grip!"

Nicolas glanced at Jacklyn, eyebrows raised. She shrugged

while David held his painful cheek.

"It's open." Nicolas stood and pulled the chain in loops. "I can't do—"

"Yes! Let's get away from here, quick!" David grabbed the chain bundle and turned south. He fell on his knees and got up again to stumble the next steps. "I know there's a road somewhere. I heard trucks pass by."

Nicolas exchanged glances with Jacklyn when he stowed his knife again. Neither believed David's words. Nicolas shouldered the backpack again, and they followed David, who tripped over branches and hardly kept on his feet.

Chapter Twelve

Matthew chewed on a pen until Jason frowned at him. Just to be ornery, Matthew rewarded himself with another cup of coffee. He wanted to brew a new pot, but Jason took the coffeepot out of his hand, accompanied by a very strict look.

Matthew lifted his hands and returned to his desk, sipping the excellent brand. To anger Jason, he smacked his lips delightedly. "How did the killer find them? What's his MO?"

Jason spooned coffee into the filter. "Start with victim number one. How did he get to her?"

"Amber Fowler." Matthew skipped through the pages, careful not to spill coffee across the file. "She had a child at the age of nineteen, but graduated with the best grades and became a doctor of medicine. She was a well-known doctor in Westbrook." He pulled the yearbook of her graduation and those of the following years. "Ah, that's it. She has her picture in the high school's hall of fame — with her maiden name and a short bio, including her name after marriage." He looked up. "That was easy."

Jason watched the first drops of coffee fall into the pot before he turned around. "The killer catches her and tortures her to reveal the names of the remaining members of the clique." He sat down. "Once he has the names, he finds the addresses. After that, he spies on them and strikes when he's ready." Jason frowned. "But —"

"But he takes his time. It's not like he rushed through it and killed a woman a day. There were weeks in between. Why wait?"

"Other obligations?"

"You mean he's got a daytime job?"

"If so, it's a job with a lot of spare time."

"Someone who drives around in a truck." Matthew grinned. "That explains why he could transport his victims quickly and without being seen. Maybe he's a one-man company. Deliveries from state to state."

Jason nodded. "Or any other occupation that grants him spare time whenever he needs it. He's not employed at a company with regular working hours and twenty days of vacation a year." He looked at the whiteboard. "He took his time because he had to be elsewhere, but when he got back to a victim, he made sure he wasn't being watched by neighbors or colleagues at work."

"Maybe he needed more time to locate one of the women." Matthew pointed at the map. "Here, look—Shelley Morgan lived in the woods, in a town called Livermore. I bet this wasn't easy to find." He read the lines about her murder again. "But then she was killed while she visited Portland. What a bad coincidence!"

"It's possible he changed cars. The victims lived in different towns. It was not until the third murder that the homicide squads informed each other and focused on him."

"Unfortunately, they didn't call the FBI sooner."

"Right. Without the query, we wouldn't know of him at all."

"A cross-state serial killer." Jason got up when the coffee maker gargled with the last drops. "Do you think he'll go for Hazelton?"

"I'm wondering what Margie Winters wrote to Timothy in that letter. I understand the part with the apology to her first-born son, but if she was so frustrated with her old friends, I bet she told him more about the circumstances, just to make her apology more believable."

Jason returned with a fresh cup of coffee, looking pleased like the Cheshire cat. "Then he squeezes Terry Winters for information to confirm what his mother wrote and sets out." Jason huffed. "That's a lot of criminal energy." He put the cup on a coaster. "If you're right, he could be in the system already."

"We know that his childhood—compared to that of Terry's—wasn't the best. If his adoptive parents had told him about his family and his adoption he would've had a chance to search for his mother when he was old enough. Remember Terry's words—when Timothy first learned of his mother, she was already dead, and he had no chance to meet with her, ever."

"Which leads to the fantasy that—if he had known her—his life would have been much better. Is that what you're saying?"

Matthew nodded and reached for the pen again. Upon Jason's glare, he dropped it, smiling. "Do you think it was enough for Timothy to sharpen a knife?"

"Let's talk with his adoptive parents when we know his real name. Maybe they can shed a light on their son."

Keith had no trouble following the footprints the couple had left in the soft soil. The hunt became more difficult along the rocky parts of the way, but by then he'd understood they were going straight south. He admired the man's ability to keep going in one direction. When he looked around, he realized the couple was heading toward the area where he had left the man who had come with the wonderful Rebecca, and he increased his speed. He couldn't tell why, but he didn't want the fugitives to find the man he had tethered, if only to keep them from saving him. The traitor deserved what he had planned for him — to die of hunger and thirst after he had cheated on the woman he pretended to love.

After he had bound Rebecca's hands and taken her away in the van, Keith forced her to tell the entire story. She didn't want to talk at first, but a believable threat convinced her, and Keith learned of David Callahan's run for fame and that he never stopped writing stories, not for anything in the world.

Grudgingly, Keith admitted that the reporter was clever. He was a cheater, too, a man who didn't deserve to live. He let Rebecca tell him everything she knew about David and concluded that the last story the man wrote would be done with a twig in the soil around his prison.

He didn't tell Rebecca. Upon her urgent and tear-stricken plea to let David live, he agreed that he wouldn't kill him. In return, she should not try to escape from the cabin where he took her to live with him. She was irritated and asked what he wanted to do with her. Keith told her that she would find everything she needed — food, water, wood for the fireplace. She wouldn't be missing a thing. She was skeptical and afraid of him. Keith couldn't find words to console her and hoped his mother's spirit would guide him on how to bond with that wonderful woman so that he had a partner again. Rebecca seemed to be such a nice and loving woman, despite her outbreak against her former lover. She deserved a man who took good care of her.

He showed her the cabin and asked her to take off her shoes. Rebecca tried to run away. He caught her, took her shoes, and told her she'd better stay where she was safe. Without shoes, he explained, she wouldn't be able to walk more than a mile before her feet bled. Rebecca thrust a stone at him, screaming that she would find a way. He replied that he would return as soon as possible.

His journey to Portland had been meant to buy her a gift at

the airport, but he got distracted. Keith remembered the Hayeses and his interest in them. Now he wished he had paid more attention to Rebecca's needs. He wouldn't win her over if he showed up empty-handed. Gifts, so his mom had claimed, made a relationship worthwhile. The man had to pay attention to the woman's needs.

Deeply sighing, Keith climbed down the rock formation. Soon he would find David chained to the tree, and he hoped he was already dead.

David sat on his butt, breathing raggedly, and ran a hand through his hair. He tried to get back on his feet and sank down again. His weakness made him crazy, and he wished for nothing more than to get out of these damn woods.

"It can't be far," he whispered. "I know that I heard trucks." He was desperate to make Nicolas and Jacklyn understand. "I know it. There must be a road." He could tell by their exchange of glances that they didn't believe him. He didn't know whether he believed himself. He cursed his weakness and his kidnapper—and the entire situation that kept him from writing.

His rescue appeared like a miracle, and he poked himself to find out whether he was hallucinating and was still tied to the tree. The chain in his hand was real enough, and it was heavy. He wished Nicolas had opened the lock at the cuff, but then thought that this was the reminder of his misery. Maybe he should keep it until the TV reporters had shot their pictures and asked the first questions about his time in the woods and how he felt.

However, David felt the weight of the chain pull him down. He wanted to get up, to run toward the road he thought was nearby, but his legs were trembling and didn't support him. The strength he had gathered with workout and weight lifting was gone, sapped away by starvation. He begged Jacklyn to give him more of the delicious cheese and cookies. She shared with him, accompanied by the warning to eat slowly or he would puke.

He needed strength. The killer with the shaggy blond hair was behind them, running through the woods to end what he had begun. Shooting didn't seem like a bad way to die, but thirst and starvation did. He imagined the killer showing up in front of them, aiming at him first. It was a terrible image and yet one he could live with. He hadn't lied that he would go mad should he stay one more day tied to a tree. "I want to go on, but . . ." David sobbed. "The chain's heavy and I . . ."

"I'll help you," Nicolas offered.

"And I'll take the backpack," Jacklyn said.

David distrusted so much luck. He was a reporter, used to being pushed away. The open friendliness and helpfulness didn't fit his expectations. He decided to include Jacklyn and Nicolas in his report about the time in the woods. It would add a lot to the credibility to his words and stir sympathy from readers. He could conclude the first article with a plea for more support among all people, not only in such bitter times of need. He would write about his saviors and claim that the world would be a better place if everyone lends his neighbor a hand.

The lines sounded good. He wished he had paper and pencil to write them down.

Nicolas reached out to him. He was a tall and broad man with a friendly face and a fashionable short haircut. From his bearing, David assumed he had served in the army. The guy was so strong he could lift him one-handed. The woman at his side was older and by far less trained. She kept her head high, though, and concealed her tiredness as best as she could. Judging from their clothing, the couple fit the murderer's scheme perfectly. He was curious how they had come to-gether. They didn't appear to be a couple who'd met at work or at a gym. He would ask them for an interview once they were out of the woods. Right now, he had no breath left.

Leaning heavily on Nicolas, David shuffled on, hoping to hear the sound of an engine sooner rather than later.

"How did it happen that the killer took away your girlfriend? Is that his . . . usual way to deal with the couples?" Jacklyn asked, walking beside David.

Nicolas gazed at her, hoping she would get the message and stop talking. It was strenuous enough to keep David up-right.

David shook his head. "How should I know? But . . ." He slipped on a patch of thick leaves, and Nicolas caught him at the last moment. "Thank you."

"Just shut up and concentrate on the way."

The order stopped him from talking for a minute.

"Suddenly, Becca said she wished she'd never met me." He shook his head as he suppressed tears. "I'd never thought she'd regret the years we spent together."

Nicolas was intrigued by the revelation. "You think this was the flashpoint why the kidnapper took away Rebecca and left you behind?"

David renewed his grip on Nicolas's shoulder. "Yes! After that, he claimed that I wasn't worth any woman, that I was scum that should become fodder for worms." He shuddered violently. "It was about to happen. I don't know whether I'd have survived another night."

Nicolas kept to himself that it was surprising he had lasted so long.

"We must find her! Maybe—"

"Ssh!" Jacklyn stopped. "Listen!" Through her tiredness,

she smiled. "I hear a car on a road."

Nicolas exhaled as they slowly and carefully made their way across yet another rocky section. He kept David from falling, now that the reporter sensed the ordeal was over. On the next steep step, David lost his footing, but Nicolas had anticipated his weakness and held him by the pants belt. When David collapsed, Nicolas turned around, bent down, and lifted him across his shoulder. He hadn't anticipated the man to be lightweight. Maybe it was due to the extreme stress he was under, but Nicolas didn't feel burdened. He moved on, hardly losing speed.

Through the trees, he saw the rough pavement of the country road.

"You made it," Jacklyn said under her breath. "You really brought us this far."

Nicolas glanced at her tired face, knowing that only her strong will kept her going. "I told you I'd do everything for you."

"Even find a way out of this mess." Tears trickled down her cheeks. "You are a wonderful man."

"Thanks for the praise." They stopped on the shoulder. Never before had Nicolas been so happy to see a sign of civilization. "I'll wait with David in the shadow. You'll stop a car."

"Why?"

"No one stops for a guy like me," he replied, smiling lopsidedly. "Not the way I look. I tend to intimidate people. They'll stop for you, though, and you delay the departure so that we can join you."

"All right." She made a stumbling step forward, bracing for the task.

"You can do that." Nicolas remained behind and let down David, who was still unconscious. He pitied the reporter. It must have been horrible to be left behind with nothing but a small bottle with water, knowing the end would come slowly and painfully.

Nicolas held his breath when — after fifteen long minutes — a dark blue transporter came along. Jacklyn waved her hands, looking pitiable. She even stepped on the road so that Nicolas held his breath, afraid the driver would run her over.

The transporter slowed down, then coasted to a stop on the shoulder. Nicolas crouched to have a look at the bearded driver. He was an African-American in his twenties, wearing glasses and an irregular beard. He was dressed in a checkered shirt, brown pants, and a baseball cap. He left his vehicle immediately when Jacklyn collapsed at his fender.

"Clever girl," Nicolas mumbled.

He turned to pull David on his shoulder again. Out of the corner of his eye, he saw movement behind one of the thick tree trunks and knew that the killer had caught up with them.

Matthew was putting on his jacket when the phone rang. Jason had already left, and for a second Matthew hesitated, then took the call.

"This is Agent Nichols. The hospital just called me. Carla Demasio died fifteen minutes ago."

Matthew wiped his beard. "Damn it. Any clues about the crime scene?"

"It's obvious she wasn't killed where she was found. CSU found cement under her soles and in her clothes and hair, but it's not a rare brand that permits drawing the conclusion of its use or where it was used."

"Any fingerprints from the killer?"

"No. She was wrapped in a cheap tarp, and the killer must have worn gloves."

"A dead end."

"Not yet. She also had wooden splinters embedded in her

fingers as if she had clawed at something. The lab's still examining them. We checked traffic cam footage, but the killer was clever — this area isn't covered or the cameras don't work. The cameras are not maintained, so it seems. It was a miracle she was found at all — a tourist took a wrong turn and ended up in this alley. In any other situation, she wouldn't have been found until tomorrow or even later."

"Please, keep me posted."

"I hope you'll find this bastard."

"Me, too."

Matthew put down the receiver and was glad he would come home to a dog that was happy to see him and would brighten his evening. He decided to stop after the second beer tonight.

"Hurry!" Nicolas shouted as he struggled to lift David's limp body. His attempts at shaking him awake were in vain. "He's coming! Get inside! Now!"

For the life of him, Nicolas wouldn't watch the killer take away Jacklyn. He saw the man with the unruly blond hair appear from behind the tree and raise his gun. A cold shiver ran down Nicolas's back. Grunting with strain and bracing for the inevitable pain in his shoulders, he hoisted David across his shoulder. Jacklyn was talking with the driver, who knelt beside her with a water bottle, appearing like the saint you need on every lonely country road.

"Get inside the car!" Nicolas shouted again.

Jacklyn looked up, let the stranger help her up, and explained in clipped words what was happening.

The driver paled. "A madman? Are you nuts? What's this about?"

"Just take us out of here!"

Nicolas had the impression he heard the killer running

downhill while he aimed. Bunches of leaves tumbled and twigs broke, and he imagined his labored breathing. Fear lent Nicolas strength. He reached the road while Jacklyn pulled open the sliding door.

"Get inside and hide!" he ordered and looked at the driver. "And you — get behind the wheel!"

The driver was running around the hood when the first shot boomed through the woods. Nicolas expelled his breath as he let David slip off his shoulder. Jacklyn cried out in terror, but made it into the cargo area.

"Down on the floor!"

Nicolas flinched, then threw in the long chain that dangled on the road.

The driver put the transporter in gear. "Ready?"

"Yes! Go!" Nicolas pulled himself inside.

Two more shots followed. One banged into the metal right beside the sliding door Nicolas hastened to close. The other one slammed inside the vehicle, but Nicolas was more concerned about Jacklyn than any damage done to the transporter.

"Are you all right? Unharmed? Jacklyn? Talk to me!"

"Yes, yes, I'm okay." She lay on the floor, shaken by weeping. "What about you?"

"I'm okay. Don't worry." He pulled her in his arms, held her tight, and kissed her with feverish longing. It was the utmost reward for the pressure they had been under and a relief beyond words.

Up front, the driver glanced over his shoulder. "What happened out there? Who shot at us?"

"I don't know, but he has followed us through the woods the whole day."

"Oh, my god!" The man's hands clenched the wheel as he accelerated and checked the mirrors. "Oh, my god. This is horrible!"

"What's your name, sir?"

"Danny. I drive fodder for horses. That's the smell, you know? Herbs and hay."

"Thank you, Danny, for stopping."

"Sure thing." He looked in the rear-view mirror. "He won't follow us, right?"

"He's on foot, so no, he can't follow us."

Danny exhaled noisily. His round face was covered with sweat. "You've been in the woods for some days, huh? Who is the other guy? Is he okay?"

Nicolas turned to David when Jacklyn shook her head.

"He's not okay," she whispered.

Nicolas flinched and hung his head. "Danny, step on the gas. Take us to the closest hospital."

Chapter Thirteen

Nicolas checked David's pulse. The injury close to his lower neck was bleeding constantly, but not bad enough to indicate that an artery had been nicked. He pressed the dressing Jacklyn handed him onto the wound. His attempts at waking David were in vain, and he could see Jacklyn's mood hit rock bottom. Though tired to the bone, she still worried for others. Nicolas wanted to kiss and hold her and tell her that she was the bravest woman on earth, *Lara Croft* be damned.

All he could do was kiss her dry lips and assure her that everything would turn out just fine.

"What a fucking vacation," she said quietly as she wiped away tears. "My parents will have gone mad in the meantime."

"Right." Nicolas admitted he had completely forgotten about Mr. and Mrs. Hollander, and he was ashamed that he hadn't been so excited about meeting with them in the first place. "They will be worried for you."

She made a face. "Just for me? You still think they don't want you around?"

"The idea crossed my mind."

"My mother will never understand that I didn't marry up. I told her that my love life is mine, and that she can kiss my ass. She decided to stay decent and accept that I'm in love with a man who's neither a rich guy nor an influential guy." She kissed him with deep affection. "But a guy who's able to save me in the woods, keep his head up, and manage to reach civilization without running in circles."

"Thanks for the praise."

"Don't be so modest."

"Right now, I'm not modest, just dirty and tired. And thirsty, not to mention. Do we have some water left?"

She handed him the bottle and took over keeping pressure on the wound. "He'll make it, right?"

"I hope so." Nicolas emptied the bottle, thinking that water had never tasted so sweet. His next thought belonged to the maniac, who had been denied his latest victims. Nicolas wondered what he would do, where he would turn to, and whether he would hurt other people until the police caught him. The agent in him wanted to contact the colleagues from the Portland field office and have this part of the woods thoroughly searched until the killer was found. Maybe David's girlfriend was still alive.

"Take a rest." Jacklyn put a hand on Nicolas's arm. "Please. I can see you're already three steps ahead." She turned to the driver. "Danny? How far to the next hospital?"

"I'm taking you to Rumford. They have a hospital. We're about ten minutes out."

Jacklyn leaned back against the sacks of fodder when Nicolas took care of David again. "Ten minutes." She helped herself to a swig of water. "I think I can do this."

For an immeasurable time, Keith stood at the slope facing the country road, motionless, his mind void of any thoughts. He replaced the bullets and secured the rifle, drank a swig of water, and stared at the road where the van had taken away three people he was determined to kill. They should not live when he had decided that they should die. The images of them hurrying toward the van were imprinted in his mind, and they were wrong. He had even seen the chain with which he'd tethered Rebecca's double-minded lover to a tree. How was it possible the chain broke? The man had looked weak — a weasel. Had the other one torn it apart? Hayes looked strong enough.

Slowly, regaining his wits, Keith turned to walk uphill and back to Aunt Ronnie and Joe, the Judge. He was ashamed he couldn't deliver good news. They counted on him to do the right thing. He had failed them, and failure had consequences. Always.

Rebecca came to his mind. With her lovely image, he increased his speed. He wanted to go back to her, hold her in his arms, and tell her about the day's misfortune. He wanted to hear her voice and hoped she would understand his need for a partner he could trust. His mother had been a wonderful woman, strong and yet gentle. She had never betrayed or left him alone — until that weekend she decided to stay in Portland. Keith didn't remember the reason, but his thoughts returned to the day the police had delivered the devastating news.

There was no solace for the death of a mother.

Tears trickled down his bearded cheeks. Aunt Ronnie had told him that Shelley was in heaven and looked down upon him. He believed her, because his mother's voice was in his head from time to time, delivering wisdom or just an order about what he had to do.

Thinking of the beautiful woman in his cabin, Keith hurried through the woods to reach her before nightfall.

Nicolas lived through the half hour after their arrival at the Rumford Hospital as if trying to find a way through a maze amid a psychedelic dream. Though he spoke, acted, and took care of Jacklyn, he couldn't focus, and he was afraid he missed important parts of the conversation. No matter how hard he tried, his concentration was gone. A nurse spoke about exhaustion, lack of sleep and water, but Nicolas didn't think about himself. He made sure the nurses took David to the ER right away, he gave the information about himself, and made sure that Jacklyn was examined for injuries. She needed a warm meal and a bed. Ten hours of uninterrupted sleep would be fine, too. She had barely made it into the hospital, and he saw her fall asleep the moment the examination was over.

"Sir, sit down before you fall down."

The friendly nurse's voice rang through his trance. He looked up, understanding finally that she'd spoken to him. She urged him to sit on an examination couch.

"Your wife told us you were shot in the woods."

"Yes." He tried to take off his long jacket. The nurse helped him, for his strength was reeling. "A gunshot, old rifle . . . it's a surprise he hit me at all."

The nurse cleaned the wound and dressed it professionally. She assured him that it was only a scratch and would heal without a scar.

"I need a phone," he said, suddenly remembering his duty.

"In the hallway. Wait, sir, let me check your vitals first. You look very tired and exhausted."

"I've had easier days," Nicolas mumbled and wiped the bridge of his nose.

She smiled. "You can lie down if you wish."

"Thanks, but, no. If I put my head on a pillow, I'll be asleep in seconds." He watched her taking his blood pressure. "I need to call the FBI."

"Sure. You should make this a short call. It's important that you drink and eat and rest. You're close to collapsing, no matter how you feel right now." She handed him a cup of water. "The adrenalin that brought you here will drop."

Nicolas nodded, too tired for a conversation. He made it

back to the hallway, found the number of the FBI field office, and told the agent in charge everything he remembered about the kidnapping, the van, the cabin, and the looks of their kidnapper.

"We've been to this place," Agent Drexler said, flabbergasted. "I remember that hole in the ground, and I remember the man." Paper rustled. "Keith Boswell."

"That must be him."

"His cabin was clean, and the tires of his van didn't match the prints we had found. He must have changed tires after the kidnapping. CSU couldn't identify any fibers or hair from the victims, either, but he claimed he'd had it washed after transporting oil and diesel. He said one of the canisters leaked. That appeared to be true, since the van still reeked of it. He's more creative than I thought. How are you?"

"Bone-tired. We rescued David Callahan, a Bangor newspaper reporter. He had been kidnapped with his lover, Rebecca, no last name. She could be somewhere, still alive, but she wasn't at the kidnapper's hideout when we were there. I looked into the cabin. It was empty. He took her away somewhere while Callahan was still locked up. That must have happened a day prior to our kidnapping. Since the kidnapper came back the same day to take Callahan away, Rebecca must be in the vicinity, either alive or dead."

"All right. I'll send my men up there at once. We'll search the entire area with all available men."

"Talk to an elderly couple—Veronica and Joe. I'm sure they're somehow involved in this scheme and know something, too."

"Sure. Anything else?"

"Yes. We're in Rumford with nothing but the clothes we're wearing. Please, send us a car and some stuff—you know what I mean."

"Consider it done. Stay where you are. We'll take care of

you."

Scott Gilford was a tall man with the tendency to stoop. He was in his fifties but wore his hair long at the neck without bothering to tie it back. His gray beard needed a cut, and if he hadn't worn an expensive suit and a watch that couldn't be found from a vendor in a shady alley, Jason would have wondered whether he was meeting with a lawyer or an unannounced visitor from the street.

Contrary to Jason's assumption, Mr. Gilford accepted the judge's order without further questions and revealed that Timothy Egerton had fetched his mother's letter from his office. Judging from the thickness of the letter, it had been more than a handwritten apology. Timothy had taken the sealed letter and left the lawyer's office without opening it. He appeared shaken by the revelation that his deceased mother had left him anything, even if it was only a letter.

Timothy had been polite but agitated, like someone who wanted to be elsewhere and fast. The lawyer assumed Timothy would have walked to the next coffee shop to read what his mother had written. He could name date and time of the delivery and showed Matthew and Jason the receipt. Upon Timothy's request, the lawyer had established contact between the half-brothers, claiming he didn't see any harm done. He didn't know Terry Winters, though, but stated that it had been Terry's decision to contact Timothy at all. The brief conversation on the phone had been meant to inform him about Timothy's existence only. However, Terry had appeared eager to learn of a sibling.

Mr. Gilford handed the agents the addresses of Timothy Egerton and his adoptive parents, Clarissa and Walter Egerton, and concluded by saying he'd had no further contact with Timothy.

Jason left his calling card with the distinct note that he should call the FBI if he remembered anything else about Margie's first-born son.

Outside, Matthew called for an HRT to raid Timothy Egerton's place immediately and report if they arrested the suspect. The next call went to Portland to help the FBI team identify the possible suspect should he try to get to Clifford Hazelton.

"Off we go to the parents," he said when he slipped into the passenger seat. "Do you think you can ever let Nick drive again when he's back?"

"Once he's back — and I pray for his safe return — he can drive as often as he wants."

Nicolas felt as if he were surfacing from a place deep under the sea where quietness and peacefulness ruled. He opened his eyes to the bleak surroundings of a hospital room and the smell of disinfectant. He sat up slowly, aware of his bruised shoulders. His muscles were still cramped and aching. Even the move to fetch the water glass from the nightstand hurt.

Taking a deep breath, he looked to the other side. Jacklyn lay in the second bed, sleeping. She had the cover pulled up to her nose, and he could only see her tousled hair. She had never looked lovelier. Knowing that she had survived the ordeal of their escape made all his pains worthwhile. He wanted nothing more than to hold her and make sure she was alive. When he closed his eyes, the last minutes of their escape passed by, and his heartbeat accelerated. He didn't know of a worse scenario than the possibility of his loved one being shot by a lunatic.

Nicolas didn't recall precisely how he'd made it from the hallway to the room the previous evening, and who had helped him undress. Since he wasn't hungry, he must have eaten prior to going to sleep. He racked his brain until he put the pieces together. The doctor had explained that they needed rest, but that they hadn't suffered badly from the days in the wilderness. Their suffering had been much shorter and less severe than the torture David Callahan had endured. Nicolas learned that the reporter would need weeks to get back on his feet.

Nicolas understood that Agent Drexler had delivered two traveling bags during the night. Suddenly, he was eager to start into the day and call for news. Getting up was a hard task, and he sat on the edge of the bed, catching his breath. He was used to training hard and often, but the flight through the woods had taken its toll. He made it to his feet, but barely reached the table to have a look at the clothes. Panting, Nicolas cursed his stiffness. He was glad Jacklyn didn't see his grimace and how he fought to manage the few steps.

"You're already up?" Jacklyn asked drowsily.

He turned with the underwear in his hands. "Agent Drexler delivered fresh clothes for us."

"Forget about them. Come under the covers. I need you here with me."

He followed her invitation and snuggled close to her warm body. Gently, he caressed the back of her head and kissed her lips. Despite the muscle aches, he had never felt so exuberant in his life. "I love you so much. I'm so happy you're okay," he whispered.

"Same to you. I can't recall how often I thought we were done for."

"I told you we were going to make it."

She kissed him with feeling. "You were the optimist, Nick. I was breaking down."

"No, my love, you are the bravest woman I know." He wiped tears off her cheek. "You held out. I'm so proud of you."

Jacklyn wept in his arms, and he was relieved they had survived the terror and the shots. The memory would haunt him for a long time. He hoped he would never again come into such a dreadful situation.

"We need to make some calls," he said quietly after a while. "You should tell your parents you are okay, and I want to know if the FBI caught the killer."

"I don't want you to leave."

He kissed her brow, admitting that he wanted to stay in bed and forget about the obligations that were waiting for them. It would be so much easier to leave everyone in the dark and go on a vacation. "I'll take sick leave when we're back in DC, okay? I'm not going back to work right away."

She looked up to him. Her compassion touched him deeply. "You are injured, Nick. You deserve a week off, if not more. I saw how you are moving. You're in pain, and that won't go away in two days."

He didn't say he'd had worse. Instead, he remained with her for another half hour until there was commotion on the corridor. He heard phrases like *The story of the year* and *That will hit the media like a bomb.*

Jacklyn smiled. "I think David Callahan woke up and alerted his paper."

"You bet." He disentangled from the cover and dressed. "Agent Drexler delivered a cell phone. Take it, call your parents, and calm them down."

Jacklyn pulled the cover up across her chin again. "I don't want to do anything. I guess I'll make that one call and go back to sleep."

"You do that." Nicolas was still overwhelmed with bliss. He kissed her again, left her the phone, and shuffled to the hallway once more.

Agent Drexler told him they were searching the area of Keith Boswell's cabin, but hadn't located him so far. They had secured evidence in the shed — tires and tools. They were breaking into the cabin in the hope of finding more clues to Boswell's doings.

Nicolas watched the TV crew carry their cameras and equipment toward David Callahan's room where a throng of people was gathered. They all spoke simultaneously, a cacophony of shouted questions and few answers. He wondered whether David enjoyed the media attention and if he would make a fortune out of his misery. A nurse was already on her way to quiet the mass.

Nicolas dialed Jason's office number, but the call redirected to his cell phone. "Hey, it's me, Nick."

He heard Jason expel his breath. "Buddy, you're free? That's the best news since Elaine accepted my proposal. Okay, and the news of her being pregnant. How are you? How's Jacky?"

"We escaped by a narrow margin, but we are okay. Currently at the hospital in Rumford. Weary, tired — we'll need some time to recover, but . . . it's over. They're searching for the kidnapper."

"When Sullivan told me about the kidnapping, I was mad with worry. How did you make it?"

Nicolas summed up the events and concluded, "The FBI Portland is searching for Keith Boswell as we speak and hope to locate him close to his cabin. He's a man born in the woods, and I wouldn't be surprised if he slipped away from them. He knows everything, and he's an excellent marksman. It's . . . pure luck that we escaped." Nicolas ran a hand through his hair. "What about you?"

"Did you say *Boswell*?"

"Yes."

Jason cleared his throat, and Nicolas imagined him rustling through file pages. "I have a murder victim by the name of Shelley Boswell, maiden name Shelley Morgan. She lived in

Livermore, but was killed during a visit in Portland."

Nicolas made a step to the side to have a look at the large map at the wall. "That's in a fifty-mile radius. Livermore, Rumford. We escaped near a town named Byron. That's not a coincidence. When was the woman killed?"

"Fifteen months ago."

Nicolas massaged his forehead, trying to find the connection while more reporters marched by in hope of catching the news for the noon update. Two more male nurses came running to tell the men and women that this was a hospital and not a news conference room.

"The reporter we rescued talked about a series of kidnappings in the Portland area. They started about fourteen months ago. Contact Agent Drexler in Portland and check with him whether your case and his have congruencies other than the name of a victim."

"Will do."

Nicolas heard Matthew's honey-soft voice in the background. "Say hello to my fellow agent."

"He's a coffee moocher."

Nicolas laughed about Jason's grumpiness. "And what's new?"

"Funny. How can I reach you when I have news?"

"I'll call you. Right now, I want nothing more than go back to bed."

"I can agree to that."

Jason switched off the exuberance about his partner being free again when they parked at the curb close to the home of Mr. and Mrs. Egerton's neat house. He sat for a moment, imagining how little Timothy had grown up in the suburb, not knowing of his biological mother but thinking he was the child of Clarissa and Walter. He couldn't imagine the young man's shock when he learned that he came from different parents.

Upon Matthew's knock on the door, an elderly woman with gray hair opened it. She wore a simple dress with a flowery print and brown, worn-out sandals. Her face appeared hardened by more sad days than bright ones, and her voice was soft, an apology to accusations Jason hadn't uttered. While she put a strand of her shoulder-length hair behind her ear, she invited them to sit in the kitchen, since the living room was under construction.

Mr. Egerton, a broad-shouldered man in his late fifties, sat at a large scratched dining table, munching cookies and drinking coffee. He was wearing an old knitted sweater and jogging pants and appeared absorbed in the newspaper's front page. Briefly, as if visitors didn't concern him, he looked across his reading glasses when Matthew and Jason introduced themselves.

"What do you want?" he asked, his mouth full. He ordered his wife to pour him another cup of coffee.

"We want to know about your adopted son, Timothy." Jason pulled his notebook and pen.

"What do you want from him?" Mrs. Egerton asked, stopping with the pot in mid-air. "Is he in trouble?"

"Wouldn't be surprised," Mr. Egerton mumbled.

Jason was in a good mood, but still his fist was desperate to get in the man's face, if only because of the imposed disinterest. "We don't know that yet. Please, tell us — when did you see him the last time?"

"That was months ago," Mr. Egerton said with a dismissive gesture. "Liz, would you mind pouring coffee instead of holding tight to the pot?"

She hurried to oblige and set the pot down on the table. Her look told of fear of the news to follow. "Do you want coffee, too, agents?"

"No, thanks. Do you have any contact with your son?"

"Not really. He's not someone who comes home every weekend to have a chat with his parents."

Mr. Egerton slurped and put another cookie in his mouth. His face was tanned and full of wrinkles. The three-day stubble didn't suit him, and Jason assumed he had a day off or didn't work at all.

"Tell us how Timothy grew up."

When he put down his reading glasses, Mr. Egerton leaned back and crossed his arms, looking annoyed. "I won't tell you anything. Tell us why you come to pester us."

"Your son's the main suspect in a murder investigation," Matthew said. "We need to know about his whereabouts, his job, his cars, his friends, and where he likes to hang out."

Mrs. Egerton sat down with tears in her eyes. "Tim? A murder suspect? But that's impossible!"

Mr. Egerton didn't appear touched. He pursed his lips. "Let me tell you this. We gave this poor abandoned child a home and raised him as if he was our own son. You might think he'd be grateful, right?"

"But he was not?"

"He was rebellious. He needed a firm hand."

"You mean he received a conservative education?"

"Listen, agents. He had a wonderful childhood, believe me. When he was old enough, I told him how to work and to work hard. The young people these days are soft, but you don't survive in this country with all its competition when you're soft. I stick to it, whether you like it or not. A young man needs a firm hand."

Jason felt his hackles rise, but it was Matthew who asked,

"Did your education involve that firm hand more than figuratively?"

"Are you insinuating that a slap now and then turned him

into a criminal?" Mr. Egerton put his fleshy hands on the table, staring at Matthew with an intensity that was meant to cow his opponents.

"I'm not insinuating anything." Matthew remained calm. "I want to know whether you punished him with more than words."

"And if so?"

Matthew nodded. "Why didn't you tell him he was adopted?"

Mrs. Egerton answered after her husband's curt nod. "We had longed for a child for many years. Our child. And when we had the chance to adopt a baby, we didn't want him to yearn for someone who didn't love him and gave him away."

"You knew his biological mother?"

Mr. Egerton scoffed and silenced his wife with a gesture. "No, but when a mother gives away her child right after birth—what would be the reason other than her not wanting him? So we decided not to tell him until he was grown up."

Matthew cleared his throat and asked, "What happened when you told him?"

"He was angry at first, but I think he understood." Mr. Egerton looked at Jason and noticed his disapproval. "I wanted my son to take over business," he added heatedly. He put a plaque with the names of Walter and Timothy Egerton, address, and phone number on the table. He poked it with his index finger. "That's why I was working so hard. I wanted him to have it all—to have it easier than I had."

"But he refused?"

"He said he would open his own place." He scoffed. "And what did he do? Opened another moving company—specialized in state-to-state delivery of fragile goods. Seriously? I don't know why my business wasn't good enough for him. I had enough storage rooms—enough empty ones, too. I offered him to share. He didn't even ask for it."

Jason hid his thoughts behind a blank façade. "He moved into his own apartment and started his own company. What's the name?"

"*Egerton Good Moving Company*." Mr. Egerton got up and snipped a calling card across the table. "Here. That's his business. He gave me that when he had them printed. I don't know if it's still valid. Honestly, I don't want to know. He's an ungrateful brat. We did everything for him. I worked my ass off so that he had a pretty childhood, could attend school, and go to camps. And when it's time to shoulder responsibility, he's off, gone!" He pulled up his nose, ignoring his wife's pleading looks. "Yeah, maybe he was pissed with me that I hadn't told him about his mother. But what would have changed? She might've been a junkie, for all I know. Who knows if she's still alive?"

"She isn't," Matthew said. "His mother committed suicide eighteen months ago. Timothy never had a chance to talk to her because you denied him the information."

Mr. Egerton grunted something unintelligible while Mrs. Egerton started to weep.

"Tell us everything you know about your son's environment," Jason demanded. "About his company's status, his trucks, his preferred bars, or if he has any friends. We need to find him."

His phone rang, and Jason got up to take the call in the hallway, looking at the wall decoration. All pictures with his adopted parents showed Timothy looking seriously into the camera while the snapshots with his friends at birthday parties or at the pool portrayed him as a happy kid. He wondered how many reappearing *firm hands* Tim had come to know during his younger years.

"The suspect wasn't at home," the HRT leader declared. "We searched the vicinity, and police officers are going from door to door to ask about his whereabouts. CSU arrived to take the place apart."

"Thank you."

"You're welcome. I'll send you my report ASAP."

Jason returned to the kitchen and sat down again, shaking his head briefly to let Matthew know the result of the raid.

"Tim was always an independent character." Mrs. Egerton sighed. "Maybe too much. When he turned sixteen and had a driver's license, he spent more time with his friends than with us."

"Do you know the names of his friends?"

Mr. Egerton scoffed again, looking at Jason and Matthew as if they expected him to recite a Shakespeare play. "He didn't tell us, okay? He went away, came back to sleep, and went off again. That's why I call him ungrateful. He was never a son who would support us, not even when we needed him."

"Needed him? In what way?"

"The company's reeling, okay?" Mr. Egerton took the coffee mug but didn't drink. "Hard competition, too few workers. It's not easy these days to make money. He could've helped, but he didn't." He drank and set down the mug forcefully. "See — that's when you know that the child's not your own blood. Our kid wouldn't have left us out in the rain."

The conversation continued fruitlessly for a few minutes. Matthew left his calling card should Timothy contact them. The agents left the house.

"If it wasn't for Nick's safe return, I would be raging with anger right now."

Matthew grinned and lit a cigarette. "Yeah, I imagine you like a raging bull, taking Egerton to task. Pretty picture." He leaned against the hood. "Come on, tell me about Nick's and Jacklyn's kidnapping and how they escaped. That'll lift your spirits."

165

CHAPTER FOURTEEN

U pon Nicolas's return to the room, Jacklyn sat on the bed having breakfast.

"I know this is too much for me, but I couldn't decide what I want to eat," she said looking at the arrangement of toast, fruits, yoghurt, and juice on the small table. "You got the same, by the way."

Nicolas sat down, sighing deeply. "I'm starved."

"Yes, you are." Jacklyn nibbled a piece of toast, eyeing him worriedly. "I don't know what I'd do if you'd been killed."

"Don't talk about it, Jacky, please."

"Why? Is this an FBI thing?"

"It's a police thing." Nicolas smiled despite his deep-rooted fear that one day a shooter might be even better than Keith Boswell. "Every day when we leave for patrol, we can be hurt. If you think or talk about it too much, it's like a bad omen."

"But it's for real. You were injured this time, and it could have been worse."

"But it wasn't. If you fear something, the fear will paralyze you. As a police officer, you can't back down. It's the other way around—if civilians are in danger, it's my task to save and protect them. If need be, I have to jump into the line of fire in order to save a person from harm."

"The way you say this makes me shiver—both with fear and with awe. I've known from the beginning that your job is so much more than representing the law. These days, I find it more and more difficult to let you go." She set down her cup of coffee. "I can't get over the fact that the reporter has a gunshot wound in his neck. How is it possible that the bullet missed you? I know that it missed you, but it was so damn close. Another inch . . . He might as well have shot you."

Nicolas lowered his chin, not knowing what to say. He sat on the bed and buttered a piece of toast.

"I want to know how other police wives handle this."

"I'm sure I can arrange a meeting." He listened to the sounds in the corridor, and when an all too eager reporter entered their room, he was quickly on his feet to send him away. He locked the door.

"And here you go again, ready to protect us." Jacklyn cocked her head. He wanted to see pride in her eyes, but it was shadowed by concern. She opened her arms, and he bent to kiss her. "Thank you, my great protector."

"Well, I didn't need to wrestle him. And I admit I would not want to wrestle anyone in the next few days."

"My parents arranged flights for us to DC."

Nicolas sat on the bed and continued eating. "They don't expect us to meet them in Popeville?"

Jacklyn made a face. "You're cute. My mom was beside herself with worry. Even my dad asked after our wellbeing immediately. They'll meet us in DC. Don't worry, they'll stay at a hotel. I didn't invite them to stay with us, and she didn't ask for it. I bet they'll make up for all of this their way."

"What do you mean?"

"The manor in Popeville is a luxury abode, Nick. If we can't spend our vacation there, they might send us to another resort — somewhere nice and quiet, to recover and relax."

"With them rooming next door?"

"I don't think so." She sipped juice, and slowly the sparkle in her eyes returned. "I intend to use this opportunity and ask them for a trip to Miami, or the Caribbean. Hawaii would be nice, too."

Nicolas shook his head. "I won't get that many days off."

"Let my parents handle this." She twitched her brows. "I bet they already did."

Keith heard his mother talk to him—through the leaves and the wind. Her voice was sometimes soothing, other times agitated. Right now, she told him to hurry and take Rebecca to a different location. He wouldn't want her to fall into the hands of the police officers who were warming the woods like fleas in summer.

He had been shocked to learn that men in FBI jackets, supported by local police forces, had raided the cabin he had built in his adolescence. Never before had his home been invaded by hostile forces. He thought about shooting them, but decided they were too many. If one of them called reinforcements, he wouldn't make it. Instead, he turned on his heels and ran back toward Rebecca.

She argued with him to let her go, and he saw no other option than to gag and tether her and carry her away. She didn't understand the imminent threat, and she did not yet grasp how much he needed her.

When she struggled on his shoulder, he threatened to knock her out. She was quiet now, and he made good progress, farther uphill, closer to the remote areas where a pursuit would be more difficult.

He knew of places to hide no police officer had ever seen.

Jason took off his trench coat when the telephone rang. Matthew beat him to taking the call. "Agent Fincher, you're on speaker. What do you have for us?"

Fincher's voice was dark with restrained anger. "A man matching the description of Timothy Egerton tried to attack

Clifford Hazelton on a golf course in Cumberland."

"What happened?" Matthew sat down and took notes.

Agent Fincher reported that the suspect had pretended to be one of the caddies who collect balls beside the green. When Hazelton had followed his ball to a place beside the course between trees, Egerton had pulled a knife. FBI agents had been waiting close by to ward off the attack. Though they'd succeeded and saved Hazelton, Egerton had beaten two agents and wounded a third one severely. Obviously, he had planned his escape in detail—a motor-cross bike had been waiting for him in a utility shed so that he was much faster than the agents pursuing him on foot. Though a manhunt had ensued, the suspect had fled the golf course. Traffic cameras had showed him outside on the road. He'd left the bike at a shopping center and vanished inside.

"He had another vehicle waiting at the parking lot on the other side of the shopping center," Agent Fincher said, deeply disappointed. "We issued a search for the company van but without success. We don't know what car he's driving right now. He didn't steal it, though. No report came in. He might have rented it, but if so, the rental agencies in the region don't have his name on the list. We're supervising the interstate and highways in all directions."

"You saved Hazelton," Jason said encouragingly. "Egerton won't try that again. By the way, how did he find Hazelton?"

"The same way we did. My men called every golf course and tennis court in a hundred-mile radius to find out where Hazelton resided."

Jason made a face as if this should be confidential information not handed to strangers.

Fincher understood the silence as accusation. "I know we should've been close to him, but Hazelton said he can't play golf with an agent breathing down his neck. He didn't want us close to him at all and complained he didn't want body-guards. That's how things happened. Hazelton has this . . . brazen attitude that no one will do him any harm.

"When confronted with the fact that Egerton might be his illegitimate son, he told me that he'd fathered many children when he was younger. He either acknowledged them or paid the women for an abortion. His words, not mine." Agent Fincher exhaled noisily. "He behaves like a man free of sins. Imagine that—while we chased Egerton, he wanted to continue his round. He shouted at my agents to stay away, now that Egerton fled. He didn't show any decency to my agents, who needed treatment because they had successfully protected him."

Jason imagined Agent Flincher had used up his energy trying not to jump in Hazelton's face.

"Fact is, Hazelton agreed to a DNA test. He laughed and said that we could assess a sample from his doctor. His . . . polygamy is known, so to speak."

Jason rolled his eyes. He pitied Agent Flincher for his complicated dealing with the victim. "Once we catch Egerton, we'll verify the parentage. Any idea where Egerton might be heading? His place and that of his adoptive parents are no longer safe. He won't return home."

Matthew reached for his phone indicated to Jason that he would try to call Terry Winters. Jason gave him thumbs up and finished the call with Agent Fincher after asking him to send the report and pictures.

"You think he'll go for Terry?"

"He might." Matthew let it ring, but the call went to the mailbox. He left a message to call back the FBI immediately after listening to the message.

Jason reached the kindergarten principal and got the information that Terry had taken a two-day leave without further explanation.

"Harold's birthday," Matthew said, snapping his fingers. "Terry told us about it—he's going to give him the cell phone as his birthday present. If he's celebrating with his partner, he won't answer the phone."

They tried to reach Harold, but without result.

"Egerton can't be back from Portland." Matthew stood and with a glance to his watch shook his head. "It's an eight-hour drive, even if he speeds. He won't fly back. He'll know that we monitor the airports. Private airfields are a possibility, but they have to send their flight route to the controller. We could catch him when he lands. He won't risk that."

"Where do you want to go?"

"I'm sending uniforms to Terry's house in case he or Egerton show up. I'll drive to Harold's home, see if they return."

Jason sighed, but accompanied him toward the garage. "Don't you think he'll try and go for Hazelton one more time? Now that he knows the man has protection, he'll be more innovative."

"That's one possibility. On the other hand—imagine his frustration that he couldn't get to the man he considered his father. He needs to vent."

"You think in his frustration he'll go for the half-brother?"

"Yes. He assumes Hazelton will be well protected for several days, even weeks. His half-brother isn't. Terry had the beautiful childhood and everything Timothy missed, and he talked freely about it. If I had to guess, Egerton was jealous from the beginning but needed Terry for details. So he became his friend. As we learned, Terry is easy to persuade and easy to intimidate." Matthew eased on the passenger seat. "Now that we know about Egerton, he's cornered. But he'll go for one last act of revenge."

While exchanging kisses, Jacklyn made it into the practical

and least stylish clothes she had ever worn, provided with a small calling card by the FBI field office in Portland.

"You're still the most beautiful woman I know," Nicolas whispered in her ear and nibbled her earlobe so that Jacklyn giggled.

"You are laying it on thick."

"I have to." Nicolas pulled down the dark blue sweater and caressed her ribs up and down. "I can't stop touching you. I think I'll accompany you everywhere you go, just to have my hands on your body all day."

"That might be embarrassing." She cupped his face with her hands and kissed his lips. "You are a charmer. And a life-saver."

"That's a story we can tell our . . . friends." His kiss was meant to cover the second of hesitation, but she knew and parted with him.

"Kids? Are you talking about kids?"

Nicolas wished he hadn't said a word. Now that Jason's wife, Elaine, was expecting a child, the thought of starting a family crossed his mind now and then. Usually, he put it away, citing the argument that it was a mistake to have kids in his line of work. Jacklyn wasn't talking about a family, either.

"Not really. Just a saying." He ran a hand through her hair, but avoided her look. "Let's get dressed. Agent Drexler said he'd send a car."

"I understand that a . . . life-threatening experience makes you think about the value of our relationship and yet—"

"No. It's all right. I'm happy with what I have."

A nurse came into the room, an apologetic smile on her lips. "Mr. and Mrs. Hayes? Mr. Callahan would like to talk to you. He can't come here, so . . . would you mind coming to him?"

"Only if he's alone," Jacklyn said. "I don't want to have a

bunch of reporters take our pictures and listen to every word we say."

"No, no. He's alone. The press left a few minutes ago, but before he goes to sleep, he wanted to thank you, I think."

Nicolas raised his brows and agreed to the meeting when Jacklyn nodded.

David lay propped up on a thick pillow, fed via IV through a vein in his left hand. A heart monitor beeped to his right. His gaunt face was almost as white as the linen, but his smile held warmth, and his eyes were lively. A thick dressing covered the left side of his neck and the upper shoulder. Although he was being provided with everything he needed, he looked and sounded exhausted.

"Hey, nice of you to drop by. I was afraid you had already left." He reached out, and Nicolas shook his hand.

"Close to leaving. We're packing up."

"I thought so. I wouldn't want to miss the chance to thank you personally. Without you, I would have died at that damned tree." He made a face as if to hold back tears. "You saved my life, and though I'm so eloquent at times, I don't know what to say to the man who was there when I was in dire need."

"I hope you'll recover soon." Nicolas's gaze fell on the chair on the right side. "You still have the chain?"

"A reminder," David said with conviction. "I will never again set out and risk my life or that of others. Unfortunately, the police haven't found Rebecca yet. Or do you have other information?"

"No, I'm afraid not."

"An FBI agent was here to talk with me. They're searching for Rebecca and the killer in the woods. Now that they know his name and whereabouts, I hope it's but a matter of time. And I pray that they'll find Becca alive."

"We hope so, too."

David seemed to gather his wits. "I assume you were also on a vacation. What are your plans now?"

"We're going home," Jacklyn said in a tone that defied further questions.

David nodded curtly. "I didn't mean to pry. I would like to praise you for your outstanding help — by name, if you permit me to do so. I would be honored to write the story and include you."

"No." Jacklyn stood at the foot of the bed, glaring at David as if he had made an indecent proposal. "I don't want reporters on my doorstep like they came to you. We were happy we could help, but that's it."

David smiled, despite her negative attitude. "That's why I was asking. I have to deal with the media every day, and even more now. Once the killer is caught, there will be questions concerning the circumstances of his arrest, and I heard that you, Nick, had to do a great deal with it. You're a federal agent."

Nicolas shrugged.

David took his silence as an invitation. "Did you undertake this journey for a kind of covert operation?"

"No, we didn't." Jacklyn stood beside Nicolas. "We were hoping for a beautiful vacation, and all we got was a kidnapping and fear of death. I'm happy we survived and that you survived, too, but that doesn't give you any right to use our names or even insinuate that we were on an investigation. If I find a single line about us, be aware that I'll send my lawyer to your paper."

"Aren't you being a bit harsh?"

Nicolas thought the same, but he couldn't stop Jacklyn.

"I've known people like you all my life." Jacklyn held tight to Nicolas's hand, as if that would keep her from jumping in the reporter's face. "Your call to the paper and the ensuing arrival of TV crews tells me that you'll use this adventure to your advantage—including the chain you put there decoratively. Do it. Become famous because you survived, but I don't want to be a part of it. Our lives are upside down because of a killer roaming the woods. If it wasn't for Nick's outstanding strength and skills, I'd be dead."

"As would I," David said quietly.

"Yes, so then respect our demand to leave us out of it."

"You do know that some people in this hospital know your names, right? Be aware that reporters will find out that you were the ones who saved me. I bet they'll also find the driver of the car that brough us here." David's look begged for forgiveness. "Even if I keep you out of my story, there will be others talking about it. It's not a little thing in this hospital when they treat people with a gunshot wound."

"I don't care about the others." Jacklyn shook her head. "For them, we're just a footnote and forgotten tomorrow. The greater story will be the killer's arrest, and I hope that you will keep quiet about us."

"I will. Promise. Believe me, Jacky, the events of the last three days changed my view of the world profoundly. I pray for Rebecca's life. Everything else comes second."

Mentioning his girlfriend mellowed Jacklyn's anger. She forced a smile. "Well, I hope she'll be found alive. We have to go."

Nicolas wished the reporter the best and followed Jacklyn into the corridor. "You saw through him pretty fast."

"My dad deals with reporters every day. If you don't give them clear orders, they pester you again and again. I'm aware that our names are known, and maybe the FBI will mention your involvement in the investigation. Maybe local reporters will get wind of that. But I wouldn't allow David to use us for his purposes."

"Whatever they may be."

She glanced at him. "Fame and fortune, I bet. Not even the worry for his girlfriend seemed real." She touched his cheek. "You are the genuine article, my love. You are as authentic as a man can be."

"I'm very close to blushing. Please, let's leave and fly home."

Keith heard the order to get his hands up. He heard the guns being cocked. He heard the many men surrounding him at the cave where he had hidden Rebecca. He thought of her well-being and that she would be lost without his protection. A warning shot rang through the air, as loud as the striking of a bell when you're standing in the bell tower. Keith stood, panting, and slowly lifted his hands in the air. His mother told him to give up and save his life, so that was what he did.

While he obeyed, he searched his mind for how the police could have found him.

A man in uniform shouted at him to lie down prone. Keith kissed the soil and deeply inhaled the smell of the woods where he had lived for so long. He turned his head to look at the treetops and the sky. Handcuffs locked around his wrists, and someone behind him read his rights while he was allowed to get up again. He didn't listen, but turned his head to the cave entrance.

Rebecca came out, crying. A police officer wrapped her in a blanket, and Keith was about to tell them that he would have provided everything a woman needed if he had the chance to keep her. She looked at him with an expression full of fear and anger. He didn't understand her yelling when all he had wanted was to have a partner at his side. Quickly, she walked away, and Keith was taken back to a main path where a police van waited to take him to town.

He looked back into the glorious woods in spring. Fresh

green everywhere, birds singing in the branches. Keith wondered where the police were taking him and whether he would ever see the woods again.

Chapter Fifteen

Egerton didn't show up at Terry Winter's home or at Harold's abode. Matthew sent Jason home to his pregnant wife, knowing she was expecting the baby within two weeks and needed company. Alone and restless, he called Sullivan to ask for permission to have Harold's apartment opened by a locksmith, claiming that both Harold and Terry were in imminent danger if he couldn't find them. He hoped for clues inside. Sullivan hesitated, told him to wait, and the line went dead.

Matthew sat in the darkness, munching on cookies Jason had left behind and drinking lukewarm water from a bottle he found behind the passenger seat.

When Terry and Harold didn't show up and couldn't be reached via phone within another thirty minutes, Matthew drummed the wheel. Senior Agent Sullivan didn't call back and was away from his desk, unavailable for a decision. Matthew didn't risk waiting any longer.

He ordered a locksmith to open the apartment and went searching for clues for the two men's whereabouts. He found a much-used address book on a cluttered desk and called the first two persons with Harold's surname. Though it was already night, both Harold's sister and his mother were awake and ready for a chat. The sister, a woman with a voice so loud she could fill an opera house, told him with laughter in between that Harold had a friend—she didn't know the man's name—with a house at Whitewood Beach, a two-hour drive south of DC, by the waterside. She guessed that Harold would spent a day or two riding or hiking with his partner, for it would be too cold for swimming. Matthew thanked her and grimaced when he put down the receiver. His ear was ringing.

He spent another forty minutes calling every person he assumed to be either friend or relative to ask for Harold's friend at Whitewood Beach until he finally spoke with the house owner, an eighty-year-old retiree with bad hearing, who told him the name and address of the exclusive resort. He concluded that the police shouldn't break anything. The house and furniture were expensive.

Matthew informed the HRT to join him for a possible manhunt, then called the security at Whitewood Beach. The elderly man at the other end of the line appeared drowsy and didn't understand the haste to get to Harold Foster and his partner. Matthew tried to explain while he drove, but wasn't confident that the private manager would act.

After the conversation, he expected Sullivan to call him, but the line remained quiet.

Terry trembled so badly, his body shook.

A moment ago, he'd been sitting with Harold on the terrace, enjoying a glass of port, and listening to the waves rolling on the beach while behind them, the CD with Al Jarreau's *Your Song* was playing. Then Harold had collapsed beside the table, and his head was bleeding. Aghast, Terry had knelt beside him to see how he could help. The same instant, someone had hit his head hard enough to numb him. He'd dropped beside his partner, unable to defend himself against the intruder. When he'd turned his head, he'd seen a giant dressed in black with a black ski mask, grunting at him to keep quiet. His vision had blurred, but he'd tried to stay conscious.

For the life of him, Terry was too shocked to utter a word.

He suffered being tethered and gagged, and the man in black shooed him toward a black transporter, keeping him upright when Terry's knees buckled. Irrationally, Terry thought that their outfits matched, for he was wearing a turtleneck sweater and pants of the same color. The man pushed him into the empty cargo area, tied his ankles with a rope, and sat behind the wheel.

Terry wished he knew whether Harold was okay, but the amount of blood had indicated a severe wound. And he could do nothing as the vehicle drove him farther away from Harold. Fearing as much for himself as for his partner, Terry whimpered into the gag, hoping against hope that both of them would survive the night.

Matthew drove like a maniac, blue lights on, siren whenever he deemed it necessary. According to the navigation system, the ride would take two hours and twenty minutes. He beat it to two hours, found the house with a white *Mercedes* convertible coupe parked on the long driveway. The sergeant of the HRT told him they were about twenty minutes out. He struggled with himself whether to wait or go ahead, and decided to do the latter.

Weapon drawn and ready to shoot, Matthew sneaked up to the house. He felt naked without a partner covering his back, but then pushed himself. He didn't expect a killer commando to raid the place but a single kidnapper and murderer who was out to find Terry.

The front door was unlocked, and Matthew proceeded with care through a huge entry hall and toward the soft music in the living room. When he rounded the corner, he saw the open door toward the large terrace. Next to the set table with glasses and plates, Harold lay on the floor, motionless. In the soft light from a lantern mounted under the protruding roof,

Matthew noticed a dark red puddle next to Harold's head. Hurriedly, yet without throwing caution in the wind, he crossed the distance and knelt beside Terry's partner to check his vitals. He was relieved when he felt a pulse, flipped his phone, and called an ambulance. He applied first aid and searched the house without result. Terry wasn't here anymore.

Matthew cursed that he had missed the kidnapper by a small margin.

Upon the arrival of the tactics team, Matthew explained the situation. He informed CSU and looked toward the next buildings, knowing it was useless to go from door to door and expect a neighbor to have witnessed the kidnapping. In early May, several houses were empty, and whoever lived here hadn't been on the street.

He told the team watching Terry's small house to be vigilant in case the kidnapper decided to show up with his victim. Heavy-heartedly, he dialed Jason's number.

"Buddy, I need your brains here. Egerton beat me to finding Terry Winters. He's gone, and I don't know where. Any ideas?"

Jason was wide awake and had the details of the case immediately like any computer with a large hard drive.

Terry listened to the sounds around—the smooth humming of the new engine, the rolling of the wheels on the road, the music on the radio. The driver whistled along to some of the songs as if he were driving a sack of flour to the next customer, bursting with happiness about his wonderful job. The transporter moved to the right, and by the slowing speed, Terry assumed they were leaving the interstate. He lifted his head, but he couldn't see more than street lamps through one of the side windows. He had no idea where they were going, and the ride took a long time.

Terry searched his mind about what he could do to escape. Constrained like this, he was in no shape to attack his kidnapper. Even without the ropes, he was no master of martial arts. During the next minutes, he pondered his tactics. Could he convince the kidnapper to let him go? Could he offer him anything that would change his mind? Was there something he wanted that Terry could provide?

At the kindergarten, all teachers passed tests of how to deal with a hostage situation—if a raging father appeared to claim the child without possessing child custody or if a madman showed up, threatening to kill them all if his demands were not met. Teachers were trained to remain calm and try to establish contact with the criminal, if ever possible.

Terry felt ill equipped to plead for his life. He was in too much fear to even think straight, let alone develop a strategy to discuss with a psychopath.

The transporter stopped. The kidnapper jumped out, slammed the door, and came around the hood. From the loud noise, Terry assumed they were in a desolate area where tumult wasn't noticed. When the sliding door opened, Terry saw into Timothy's hate-filled face.

"Surprised to see me, huh?" he snarled and opened the knots around Terry's ankles. "Get out!"

Terry obeyed, heart beating in his throat. During the ride, he had tried to scoop a pinch of hope into a thimble, but seeing Timothy's expression, he knew that a thimble would never be enough. He would die.

Timothy pushed him forward with so much force, Terry stumbled and fell hard on the concrete.

"Wimp!" Timothy stooped to grab Terry's upper arm and pull him on his feet. "Move!"

Terry looked around. The big warehouse was empty, desolated. Two neon lamps illuminated the front part. Close to the wall to his left stood a big wooden wheel chair like the ones used in nursing homes back in the days. However, there was more to it — straps and locks for arms, legs, and head. Terry shuddered with horror, the more when he saw dried blood on the floor. His stomach heaved.

"Sit down!" Timothy yelled and ripped away the gag.

"Why did you bring me here? What do you want from me?"

"Always the same questions." Timothy laughed. It was a harsh sound in Terry's ears, full of contempt. "We have to chat, my wonderful half-brother. Do you remember?" He pressed him on the chair and tied his hands to the armrests and his ankles to the footrest. "You told me a lot about mom, but not that she seethed with revenge."

"She didn't! She was happy with her life!"

"Are you sure about that?" Timothy forced Terry to lean against the headrest, then fastened his forehead with a cushioned leather strap. "She wanted her misery and her years of self-reproach put on her former friends. They should know how hard she fought to have a real life." He went back to the entrance to lower the rolling gate. Terry assumed they were in a district with storage rooms and offices, a lonely area at night.

When the gate closed, Terry had the impression that his fate was sealed.

He clawed at the armrests, mad with fear. "She was happy with Jim! She didn't want anything else! She had . . . me." Terry cast down his gaze immediately.

"You!" Timothy snorted with disgust. "Yes, she had you to pamper and spoil. How could I forget the shine in your eyes when you talked about those great days at playgrounds and that she had taught you how to ride a bike. Happy times, huh?

I grew up far away from her without her gentle touch, her love, and her support. She told me in her letter how hard it had been for her to part with me, and that she never forgave herself."

"That's a lie! She could've looked for you if she had—"

Timothy hit Terry's cheekbone so hard, Terry saw double. He was numb, and his ears rang. A second later, his cheek was on fire.

"You're a stupid brat! She couldn't just march in and claim her son back even though she knew who had adopted me! An adoption is final. She wrote that Jim had kept her from coming back into my life because of that. If she'd been alone, she would have tried!"

Terry wept as quietly as he could. He had never felt so lonely and hopeless before.

Matthew put his phone on speaker in the car. "Tell me your idea."

"Egerton needs a remote place where he can deal with his victims without being disturbed. The place must have a garage or be large enough to park a van. It should possess a good road access in case he needs to get away quickly. He's a man who wants to know it all. He's meticulous, focused—that's what Terry described when he said that Timothy wanted to know everything about his mother. He's a planner. Which means he has a hideout that's still undiscovered, even though we found Eldridge in Fredericksburg and Demasio in DC."

"We checked Egerton's home and didn't find any clue—no rental space, nothing."

"But we know that the concrete found under Demasio's soles is used inside buildings, not for pavements." Jason pondered for a minute. "Mr. Egerton told us that he took his son with him when he was old enough—taught him how to work.

Which means Egerton junior knows about his father's storage rooms intimately."

"I'll ask Mr. Egerton right away. Hang on."

"I'll get dressed in the meantime."

Matthew let it ring twenty times, but the Egertons were not at home or didn't answer the phone. He drove to their house and hit the doorbell with more force than necessary. Finally, Mr. Egerton appeared on the doorstep, a pistol in his hand.

While Terry sobbed, Timothy moved forward and backward as if listening to some piece of insane music.

"And then you came into my life! I thought I was meeting with a likeminded soul, but no, you were so soft-spoken and friendly and considerate, I wanted to puke. Still, I trusted you, and what did I get? You rat me out to the FBI! Why? Why didn't you value our friendship and kept it a secret? That's what you wanted, right? Keeping you and me a secret. You never invited me to your home so that I wouldn't know of your partner. Yes, I knew of Harold Foster pretty fast," he said, nodding when Terry's eyes widened with horror. "Do you think I'm stupid? I followed you right after our first meeting. Saw you kiss him on the doorstep. Yuk! I know you didn't tell me about him because you didn't know whether I would reject him."

Terry closed his eyes. Instead he saw Harold lying on the floor, bleeding. The bad premonition that his partner was dead took his breath away. How could anyone be so cruel and rob him of his purpose in life? His voice dropped to a frightened whisper. "Why are you doing this to me?"

Timothy scoffed. "You need to ask? You led the perfect life—parents who loved you, a good education, friends, money."

"That's nonsense. They left me nothing but some unpaid

checks."

"Do you know what?" Timothy asked, disregarding Terry's remark. "If your father wasn't already dead, I would kill him. He was the one who urged my mom to give up me up. He didn't want me in his life — probably because he thought that he would be second best, once I grew up. He claimed that it was the best decision for everyone because the Egertons had already adopted me. He decided to leave me in the dirt and convinced mom to follow his decision."

Terry needed time until he dared to speak. "It was a difficult time for her."

Timothy smacked Terry's face with the back of his hand. "Don't you dare tell me about hard times, you fag!"

Terry's lower jaw dropped, as much from dismay as from pain he couldn't cope with.

"Yeah, I know what you are. I know that the old one's not just a friend. He stakes you, right? Or is that payment for your service to him? Do you have to bend over every night so that he has fun?"

Terry pressed his lips together to keep quiet. Although Harold's and his relationship was the subject of snide remarks now and then in places where they dared to go together, Timothy's statement cut him deeply. He couldn't remember ever having felt so miserable in his life, not even after the death of his parents. He wanted to be out of the situation so badly, he wasted his strength tearing at the tethers holding him.

Timothy slapped Terry's chin, then bent to look him in the eyes. "He's an old man! Why didn't you find someone your age? Well, looks like you need the money. Isn't this why you suffer his presence? Are you a rent boy?"

Terry's voice was hoarse with fear. "How did you learn about Whitewood Beach?"

"Because you told me." Timothy stepped back like a dancer and lit a cigarette. "I listened to every word you said,

Terry-boy." He blew out smoke.

If it wasn't for the gruesome circumstances, Terry might have imagined this to be a scene from an old gangster movie he loved to watch with Harold.

"You claimed you had a rich friend with a house on the beach. A little encouragement and you blurted out all the information I needed. It's a marvelous house, I give you that. You forgot to mention that Harold wasn't the owner, but his old partner. I had to research a little bit, but then I borrowed your cell phone while you went to the restroom. You're a very orderly person. You took down notes about the numbers you saved. Harold's friend had the note about the house and even the address. Easy-peasy."

Terry had trouble comprehending that his half-brother had done nothing but spy on him and his loved ones to destroy him in the name of revenge. His parents had taught him to see the best in people. Meeting Timothy had appeared to be such a life-enhancing event that he had never questioned the man's motivation or background. Only when the FBI agents asked him about Timothy did he realize how little he knew about him. "Did you kill those women?" Terry asked quietly, facing the floor.

"You're a slow wit, huh?" He blew out smoke and seemed to enjoy the minute. "Of course, I did! Mom told me their names in her letter — in red, accompanied by details she remembered. She had hoped that they would support her in her time of need, but they told her to take the man's money and abort me! Imagine that! That's why she took the car that night. She wanted to commit suicide and leave this world, but it didn't work. And when she woke up, she was worse off — disfigured for life! And still alone in her misery."

Timothy placed his hands on the armrests and put his face close to Terry's. "That's why she gave me away. That's why her life and mine were miserable. That's why she never got over that year and never told you about my existence." He pushed off again, leaving Terry in terror of his next attack. "She wanted revenge. She wanted to let them feel how she had felt. But she left it to me, to have it done after her death."

"She would never have wanted anyone harmed." Terry looked up again into Timothy's eyes. The hatred he found was so profound that he shivered. Once more, he writhed in the tethers, but had no strength to tear them apart.

"She told me their names and how they picked on her and dropped her, finally." Timothy pulled a thick envelope from his breast pocket. Terry realized that his mother had left Timothy much more than a short hand-written apology. Timothy put out the cigarette and unfolded six tightly written pages. "See? Names, places, preferences, parents. She took it all down, trying to make it easy for me to find them."

"When did she write that letter?"

"About ten years ago." Timothy smoothed the pages in a loving gesture.

"Ten years ago, mom was very sick. The doctors didn't know whether she had an ulcer or cancer. She was at the hospital for three long weeks without knowing about her chances of recovery. She must have written the letter in those days." Terry wet his lips. "She was . . . very worried she'd die, so she might have written things she didn't mean that way."

"It's clear to me how disappointed she was in her so-called friends. She wrote, *When I was on the phone with Amber, I heard Shelley laugh in the background. Then Amber chuckled. I imagined them imitating my half-dead face and put down the receiver. After that, Shelley called me to tell me that I got it all wrong and that I shouldn't be so thin-skinned. Not everything they said was directed at me. But I knew better.* Timothy slapped the sheets of paper with the back of his hand. "See? It's all here. Her former friends had dropped her, mocked her, and told her just to live on and deal with her decision. But it wasn't that easy! I understand her."

"She wouldn't have wanted anyone harmed," Terry repeated, unable to grasp that his wonderful mom might have been out for revenge, even if it was after her death.

"Yes, she would!" Timothy stowed the letter again. "She even told me to go for my father at last. I almost made it!" He hammered his fist against the wall, howling with disappointment.

Terry wished he could slip through the tethers and vanish through a slit in the door. The terror he suffered was beyond every feeling he had experienced in his lifetime, and he had no hope that it would end soon. Obviously, Timothy had chosen a place no one would look for him. Once more, Terry's thoughts were with Harold. There were no neighbors to look for him, so no one would find him until morning — too late to treat a severe injury.

"I was so close to stabbing him! And then the fucking FBI showed up. How could they have known?" He swiveled around and grabbed Terry's sweater. "You told them about me in the first place, right?" He slapped his face again. "You put them on my trail!"

"I had to! They left me no choice!"

"Cocksucker!" Timothy went for Terry's throat. "Did mom ever mention Clifford Hazelton to you?"

"No! Never!" The pressure was so strong Terry couldn't breathe.

Timothy's voice sank to a menacing growl. "I don't believe you anymore. You tell me what I want to know, or I swear you're gonna regret it!"

Matthew didn't waste time with words. He wrested the gun from Egerton's hand and pushed the man back into the hallway with his face against the wall.

"Are you out of your fucking mind? I'm a federal agent!

How do you dare point a gun at my face?"

Egerton grunted when Matthew turned his arm behind his back. "How dare you show up in the middle of the night, bastard? I have rights!"

Matthew stowed the pistol and handcuffed Egerton before he let him turn around. He was sweating profusely and needed a moment to get hold of his professional distance. Without a badge, Matthew would have punched him in the face. When Egerton had protested, he would have punched him again and had fun doing it.

He forced his voice down. "I need to know the addresses of your storage rooms."

"Now?"

"Right away. Your son kidnapped another victim, and his life hangs by a thread. So, yes, right away. All of them, if there's more than one."

"I've got one, but it's out of town—close to Fairfax. It's much cheaper there."

"I need the address." Egerton told him where to find the map and when he had it stowed, he called Jason. After that, he released Egerton without handing back the pistol. "You can get it back if you've got a license."

He hurried to his service car and drove off, tires squealing.

"I didn't know about Hazelton!" Terry gulped in air when Timothy released him. "Believe me, I would have told you!"

Timothy straightened. "Yeah, yeah, you blue-eyed wimp." He cocked his head. "You were afraid of me from the beginning, right? I had you cowed pretty fast."

Terry lowered his gaze to the floor. He was close to wetting his pants. He had pulled the press information about the *Mutilator* and his methods right after the FBI agents left. The psychopath liked to see the victims suffer before they died. It wouldn't be long and Timothy would take a knife and mutilate Terry's face before he pressed it into his belly to watch him die slowly and miserably. The gruesome report details of *multiple injuries to face and torso, leading to a slow and painful death* clung to him like molasses. He felt sick to his stomach.

Terry racked his brain for what he could say to make Timothy understand that their wonderful mom had never wanted their sons to quarrel.

The knife appeared out of thin air and scratched Terry's thigh through the pants. The short and extremely sharp blade cut through fiber and skin easily. He cried out with surprise and pain.

"You never got to know her the way I did," Timothy said, eagerness in his eyes. He swirled the knife around his fingers. "She might have appeared sweet and harmless, even weak. But in her heart, she was a lioness. She stored her revenge plan and made sure I could put my hands on it. She relied on me to fulfill her last wishes — not on you. She saw you as a nice and prissy person, but you were never brave enough to stand up and fight. Mom saw through you and knew you would turn into a fag — not a man she could rely on." Timothy laughed as Terry broke down. "Oh, such sweet tears. Yes, she might have played understanding her misguided son, but she was disappointed. Very disappointed."

"No! This can't be! I know that she understood!" Terry screamed.

Timothy put away the knife, then unfolded the letter. "Terry is a wonderful young man, and you will surely love him. He's soft and friendly, so whatever you've got in mind, be gentle with him. He will be your companion in dark times, for he's a faithful and reliable man with best intentions. I wish you both well — everyone on his own path, might they be the same direction or completely different." He cocked his head. "I was told to do the work, and you were called soft. That's why I didn't let you in on my plan. It would've been futile."

191

"She didn't want you to kill these women. That can't be!"

"Terry, Terry . . ." Timothy put away the letter and let the knife reappear. "Every day when I wake up, I imagine how my life—and mom's life—would have been if we had been together. A family. With or without Jim. Maybe she would have parted with him knowing that I was much more important in her life than a social worker with a disreputable background. My father is *Clifford Hazelton*!" Timothy played with the knife, hypnotizing Terry so badly he cried out the moment the knife's tip pierced his right thigh and left a one-inch deep wound. "Imagine the child support she could have claimed! He's a rich old geezer with more money than he can spend. Mom would've had a much better life."

Timothy ran the knife across Terry's upper arm, cutting through the wool and the skin beneath. Terry grimaced with pain and expected the knife to hit his sternum the next moment.

"When I met Amber, I realized that all the women had profited from Hazelton and other scumbags roaming the golf club at that time. She confided in me that she had a child from Hazelton and was happy with him. Hazelton paid so she could study and become a doctor."

Terry panted, but summoned the strength to ask, "Did you ever think about mom's decision? Maybe she wanted to abort, and Hazelton gave her what she wanted—the money to do it."

The next blow was so severe Terry lost consciousness.

Matthew sped the service car across the highway, despite the drizzle that hampered his view and made driving dangerous. He informed Jason and the HRT to meet him at the warehouse in Fairfax, ready to storm the building. Upon Jason's question whether he was certain the killer would be there, Matthew admitted that it was a fifty-fifty chance. If Egerton junior had rented storage rooms under a different name or found a better place to hide his victim, they were out of options, at least for now.

Local police in Fairfax were ordered to guard the block and not let anyone pass, but they were told not to move close to the given address without the HRT present. Should Timothy decide to run, Matthew wanted a tail on him right away.

A truck changed lanes, disregarding the blue lights. In an instant, Matthew's car skidded across two lanes and made the exit, scratching along the barrels that kept cars from hitting the guardrail. Matthew cursed as much as he fought to steer the car along the ramp. He stopped at the next red light to relearn how to breathe and thank the heaven above for keeping him from serious harm.

He wished for a smoke, but didn't dare delay his ride.

Terry swallowed hard. The situation in the musty warehouse hadn't changed — only that Timothy had opened a can of beer in the meantime. He slurped noisily, looking at his victim now and then, pretending he had all the time in the world to deal with him.

Bile rose up, but Terry couldn't move his head. He would suffocate should he try to spit it out. With an effort, he forced it down again.

"She would never have wanted to abort," Timothy stated with conviction. "She told me she loved children."

"Think of it, Tim. If Amber gave birth and Hazelton supported her — why wouldn't he do the same for Margie? But mom made another decision, took money for the abortion and then, obviously, couldn't bring herself to do it. Only then did she try to commit suicide."

The knife slit open the sweater and the skin across Terry's

chest. The pain was unbearable. Terry screamed at the top of his lungs. While he panted and tried to cope with the torment, Timothy put the knife's tip into his nose and cut the nostril. Blood dripped across his lips and chin. Another cry slipped from Terry's lips, and he feared he might faint once more.

"You're probably wishing that I never lived, huh?" Timothy fidgeted with the knife like a performer in a circus. "You wish I'd never met you."

"I wish my mother had had the courage to go on living." Terry sobbed. "She was such a kindhearted person. I will never believe that she urged you to commit murder. That's impossible. Simply impossible."

"It's wrong that stupid, arrogant, and selfish people live," Timothy replied. "All the women—they begged for their lives, and none admitted that she had willingly abandoned my mother in a time of need. They claimed they had offered her to stay in contact but that mom had withdrawn from them more and more. Shelley said that she offered to meet with her wherever my mother wanted, but I know this was a lie. Shelley had moved to Livermore, in the middle of nowhere in the woods. How would she have stayed in contact, huh?"

He pulled up his nose, gazing at the blood on the blade. "Then she begged me to let her live because her son needed her and that Keith would freak out if she didn't return. The moment she mentioned her son, I stabbed her. She didn't deserve better. I bet that Keith was also a bastard son from one of those rich squares. All of them—they were looking after themselves. Spoiled brats! They came from wealthy families that had everything. They could support a daughter at eighteen with a baby. But my mother—she would've been alone. That's why she needed her friends!"

"That's why she decided to—"

Timothy put the knife's tip against Terry's throat and hissed, "She didn't want the abortion. Don't you get it? She wanted the same chance the other girls had. *They* urged her to take the money and be rid of me. It was the ambivalence that made her think of suicide."

This time, Terry stared into his half-brother's eyes, expecting the fatal stab, the one that would let him bleed to death. He took shallow breaths, not daring to blink or part his lips, knowing that Timothy was waiting for a wrong move to finish what he had begun. Sweat stung in his eyes, and the pain of the injuries seemed to increase by the minute.

Timothy blinked and took away the knife. "You know — I might even let you live."

CHAPTER SIXTEEN

The HRT leader, a man in his thirties of average height but remarkable width, welcomed Matthew at the crossroads outside the closed off block.

"Sergeant Rodriguez," he introduced himself with a hardly detectable Spanish accent. "We secured the surrounding streets, two blocks in every direction. My men are climbing the roofs as we speak. Can you give us a number of the storage room we're searching for?"

Matthew showed him the map Egerton had left him. "These two in the third aisle."

"All right. Shall we start there?

"Wait a moment, please."

Jason joined them, looking like someone who had tumbled out of bed and fallen into his car right away. Compared to his immaculate appearance at the office, he looked deranged — more like a real person than a distant FBI agent. Matthew didn't dare smile, but it was difficult.

"It's a big complex," Sergeant Rodriguez explained. "For now, we control the streets but not every aisle. We'll start with the rooms you told us and then move forward."

"He was playing here as a kid." Jason put his hands on his hips and squinted at the harsh neon lights. "He knows the area inside and out. We also know he's a planner — a man who wouldn't come here and risk being cornered." He took the map. "His father's storage rooms are in a center aisle, much too easy to surround. If he's here, he prefers an aisle with a separate exit. Here." He pointed at the last row.

"Not all of them are rented." Matthew agreed with Jason's choice. "He might hide in one of those."

"All right. We'll start with the aisle that leads to the rear alley and take it from there." Rodriguez turned away and informed his men via intercom.

Matthew looked Jason up and down, trying and failing to hide a smile. "I like your style."

"The offer to whack your face still stands."

Terry had no hope for a better ending, but said, "Mom wouldn't want us to fight. Maybe she thought I was soft, but she also wrote I could be your companion in dark times." He said with a feeble voice, "Don't hurt me, Tim, that's not what she wanted."

"Do you think she wanted you to be a wimp?"

"I don't believe she wanted you to become a killer. Did you do this before?"

"No, nothing like this." Timothy played with the knife. "This is my mission. After that, I might go to Portland. I like the city." He pursed his lips as he cocked his head. "What would your freedom be worth to you?"

Terry knew it was a catch-22 question. Timothy curled his lips into a malevolent smile as he caressed Terry's face with the tip of his knife.

"Huh? What would you do to . . . please me?"

Terry shuddered badly, and his words came out in a fearful whisper. "What would you expect me to do?"

"Oh, Terry-boy, soft, little wimp. You don't have the guts to do what's necessary." He moved away, only to rush back and cut the cloth and skin of Terry's right thigh. His voice sank to a growl. "Hazelton is still out there. I'll catch him. I'll make him bleed the way you bleed." He laughed. "You worry about your pretty face, don't you? Right. You'd make a good-looking woman."

Timothy stepped back as if to study his victim from a better angle. "When I checked you out, the idea crossed my mind that pretty boys like you bring good money on the market. I could sell you for a fortune."

Terry thought his horror couldn't be any greater, but Timothy played with his fears like a virtuoso on a piano.

He swallowed hard. "That won't work if you kill me."

"That's why I'm still thinking. I could use the money for a new start, now that the FBI knows so much about me." He frowned, turned away, and stood for a moment, listening. When he returned, yet another devilish smile played around his lips. "I have to put you up for a few days somewhere to make contact, but then . . . I bet that I could find you a wealthy owner who would play with you."

Terry realized Timothy would never let him go, but that his half-brother loved to see his anguish with every new possibility he displayed.

"We've located two persons in one of the rooms to the right," Rodriguez reported via intercom. "We're going in."

"Proceed with caution. One of them will be armed," Matthew said and held his breath when Rodriguez ordered the man to blow open the entrance.

They heard the dull sound of the lock exploding to shards, and then the sergeant's command to storm. Jason and Matthew followed behind, protected by their bulletproof vests. Behind the smoke, the officers pointed their guns at two white men in their early twenties, dressed in jeans and leather jackets, who couldn't look more shocked when confronted with a tank pointing its muzzle at their faces. Boxes with DVD players and TV sets were stacked up along the wall.

"Hands up! FBI!"

The men dropped what they had been holding and obeyed immediately. While they cursed and accused each other of being responsible, the officers pressed them against the wall and frisked them for weapons. They found sidearms, knives, and a brass knuckle.

"That your men?" Rodriguez asked though he already knew the answer.

"No." Matthew hung his head. "Damn it!"

The gangsters heard the conversation, and their eyes widened even more. "You weren't after us? Fuck!"

If the situation hadn't been serious, Matthew would have laughed about their perplexed expressions.

"Looks like we found two hustlers." Rodriguez looked up, frustrated. "Do you want us to continue the search?"

Matthew looked at Jason, who studied the map once more. "What's behind the area?"

"A strip with shrubbery and old warehouses, out of use." Matthew pointed at the front buildings. "This is the new area. The company abandoned the old one."

Jason looked at Rodriguez. "We're moving on."

Terry sensed Timothy's unrest and thought feverishly for how he could delay the inevitable. "Sell me? How would that work?"

Timothy smacked his lips, shaking his head. "Never heard of human trafficking? You live in a bubble, huh? Just your old geezer and a bunch of kindergarten kids. It was all over the news—the FBI broke up a human trafficking ring last year. Lots of goons arrested, lots of men saved. But they're still out there."

"You would hide me? Where? Here?"

Timothy moved his head left and right. "Are you trying to tell me you'll volunteer so that I don't kill you right away?"

"I don't want to die. You know that. Please, I'll do what you want." Terry swallowed down his heart, sensing a chance to change Timothy's mind. "So what would you do?"

"I've got places where no one finds—" Timothy stopped and went to the rolling gate to listen. "Fuck!" He turned on his heels and came running back, teeth bared. He held the knife in his hand, and his eyes were mad with anger. "You won't escape me like Hazelton did!"

Terry screamed on top of his lungs while the blade sped toward his body.

Behind him, the rolling gate exploded inward with fire and smoke.

Jason heard the man's scream despite the detonation. In his mind, the killer was mutilating his victim and stabbing his heart, mad with rage. Fear of coming too late lent him speed and knocked out precaution. He didn't wait for the HRT officers to announce the room was clear.

With Matthew close behind him, he entered the large storage room to see Terry Winters tied to an old-fashioned wheel chair. In the harsh light of overhead neon lamps, the blood on Terry's face and beneath the black sweater was of a screaming red and told the story of the past hour vividly.

"Oh, my god."

At the rear end of the large room, a door clanked shut.

Matthew stopped beside him, panting. "I follow Tim, you take care of Terry. Yes, you do. I run much faster than you do."

Jason bit down any comment, put up his gun, and freed Terry from the shackles. One look at the wounds was enough to know the young man's life was in imminent danger. He lowered him onto the ground, murmuring soothing words as he took off his jacket and folded it under Terry's head.

"Don't let me die," Terry whispered. "Please." He clung to Jason's arm. "I've come so far. Please, don't let me die."

Jason called an ambulance and put pressure on the stomach wound that appeared to be the deepest. If the main artery was severed, there was no hope that the medics would get here in time to save his life. He prayed with the urgency of a sinner who knows that a good deed will always be rewarded.

"What about . . . Harold?" Terry whispered.

"He was taken to a hospital. He'll make it. Hang on!" he shouted at Terry when the young man's eyes closed. "No, no, no! Stay with me! Harold lives! You must live to see him again." Blood oozed between Jason's fingers. When he turned to find help, an officer came running with a large first aid bag. "Stab wound to the stomach," Jason reported. "A moment ago, he was still conscious."

"Continue pressure. I'll take care of him."

When the medic took over, Jason held Terry's hand in his. "Hey, you can make it. You're young, you're strong. Don't give up. Do you hear me?" Jason was unable to distance himself from the victim. He cursed the circumstances that had delayed their arrival. They hadn't been able to save Carla Demasio, and Harold Foster would have been dead if the killer had wanted him out of the way. He didn't want to see Terry Winters die because of the killer's irrational revenge trip. "Listen, Terry, I'll see that Harold is taken to the same hospital, all right? So you can see him when you wake up."

He had no idea whether Terry could hear him. He was relieved when the ambulance arrived six minutes later and put Terry on a stretcher. He heard the medic deliver the vitals, and another one who contacted the hospital to prepare for surgery.

Looking at the blood on the concrete and his hands, Jason hung his head, fighting tears.

Matthew was a good agent who understood the meaning of acting by the book, but the arrest of Timothy Egerton was a hard test of law abidance. He'd only had a short glimpse at Terry's injuries, and from this he understood that Egerton had made a last attempt at taking revenge on the second born son who had lived the happy life he had been denied.

When he saw Egerton run like a hare through the shrubbery behind the warehouse, he gave all he had to bridge the distance. He couldn't remember ever having run so fast. He heard an HRT member shout behind him, and yet couldn't deviate from his path, gaze focused straight ahead on Egerton's broad shoulders. The fugitive panted loudly and wasted time by glancing over his shoulder. Matthew expected that he had an escape car waiting in the next alley and increased his effort to get to him.

Egerton slipped through a hole in the fence and ran on, passing by dumpsters and bulky waste people had left behind when the place was abandoned years ago. Matthew hurried through the hole behind him. Two HRT officers were closing in — Matthew heard one of them describing their position. They were slower due to their equipment.

Matthew caught up with Egerton at a row of old cars. Cornered, the killer turned and lashed out with his knife.

Matthew jumped out of reach. "You won't get away!"

Egerton bared his teeth, ready to strike again. Matthew grabbed the arm leading the knife, turned to the right and lifted his opponent for a forceful throw across his shoulder. Unlike in sports, Matthew let Egerton feel the impact on the sidewalk, wrested the knife from the man's hand and punched his face for good measure. Maybe his nose broke. Matthew couldn't tell because he was panting so loudly. He was astonished to find the two officers right and left of him, ready to take Egerton into custody.

Matthew straightened, deeply regretting that he couldn't whack Egerton's face any further. When Egerton was back on his feet, Matthew handcuffed him behind his back and led him toward the waiting HRT van, reading him his rights. At the van, he couldn't stop himself and knocked Egerton's head against the roof, and when Egerton protested, kicked him in the hollow of his knee.

His anger was not gone, but the killer was arrested and stowed in the van. The officer behind him grinned and nodded in appreciation.

Matthew looked around and found Jason standing in the empty warehouse where other officers were securing the van and searching for evidence. "Hey, buddy, I got him." Matthew stopped, realizing that Jason was staring at his bloody hands. "I'll get you some water to wash it off."

"If he dies, the killer will get what he wanted — they're all dead."

Matthew was nonplussed. He led Jason out of the warehouse, pondering what to say. "Terry was badly wounded?"

"Egerton stabbed him in the stomach. It was a short blade, and I don't know whether he had time to twist the blade so that . . ." He broke off, shrugging.

"He'll make it." Matthew was about to hand Jason a small water bottle, but when Jason remained absent-minded, he used the pint of water to wash his partner's hands. "He's young and in good health. And the ambulance was here quickly."

"Thanks." Jason wiped his hands along his pants and pulled out his cell phone. "He asked for Harold. I told him I would arrange a transport. Which hospital was close to Whitewood Beach?"

Matthew looked at a map on his phone and told him the name and number of the hospital. He kept his bewilderment to himself. Jason didn't seem to notice, anyway.

CHAPTER SEVENTEEN

Nicolas took a deep breath as he turned around, relishing that he'd slept in his own bed. After the ordeal of the last few days, he felt rested, and his spirits were lifting.

Jacklyn's parents had kept their word, arranged a flight back to DC, and taken care of a limousine that had fetched them from the airport. After a brief meeting with them, Jacklyn had declared that she and Nicolas were too tired to have dinner together and put her parents off to have breakfast on the weekend. Jacklyn's mother promised to talk to Sullivan and *other dignitaries* – so she claimed – should Sullivan dare to deny Nicolas at least ten days off from work. As Jacklyn promised, those words were law.

Nicolas couldn't have hoped for a better ending.

He looked into Jacklyn's relaxed face and kissed her nose, smiling when she opened her eyes with a growl.

"You're shaking me out of sleep this early? Are you nuts?"

"I wouldn't call it *nuts*, but if my mistress says so, she's probably right." He made puppy eyes at her, and her bad mood was gone instantly.

She replied with a kiss. "Are there any special reasons on your mind why you couldn't let me sleep in?" She caressed his bearded cheek. "Do you want to tell me something?"

"Jacky, would you do me a favor?"

"Anything you want."

Gently, he stroked back her hair. "When we were out there, running, trying to stay ahead of the killer, my only thought was to keep you safe, to get you out of this dreadful situation and take you as far away as possible. When Keith got so close he could have shot you, I think, my worst nightmares came true. I don't know if I've ever been so worried in my life. It was a . . . gruesome trip."

"I know."

"I gave all I had and now . . ."

"Now you want to give up responsibility."

He was astonished. "Is that okay with you?"

"I was wondering when you would ask."

"You were?"

"I can read you, Nicolas Hayes." She caressed his face. "I sense your mood, your emotions. I know how stressed out you are and that you only stayed on your feet because I needed you to take the lead."

"You knew I would ask you to tie me up?"

"Yes."

"Let me surrender to you." He kissed her gently. "I need this, I really do."

"You're lucky you've got a woman at your side who understands your needs." She slipped into his embrace, worry lines on her forehead. "He almost took you away from me. Believe me, I was as frightened as you were. The moment Callahan was shot—that could've been you." Jacky finger-combed his hair, sighing with relief. "You are the bravest man I know."

He kissed her hands and wrists. "And that brave man needs your permission to be weak."

"You give me permission to play with you throughout the day?"

He made a face as if pondering the proposal. "I'll need some food in between."

"And a glass of wine later. I understand." Jacky got on her knees and pulled him with her. "Let me shave you properly first. After that, we might discuss food and drink."

"You are the mistress."

Matthew was on the phone with Agent Drexler when Jason arrived at the office. He put the agent from Portland on speaker.

"Looks like we solved the crimes," Matthew summed up over the phone. "I'll have my report sent to you today, right after its approval by my boss."

"Wow. I'm impressed. You work on a great team, Agent Montagna. It was a weird situation. All the murders were triggered by the suicide of Margie Winters. If she had lived, none of that would have happened. That's so strange, once you think about it. Shelley Boswell's death was the worst. Egerton murdering her led to Keith Boswell turning into a couple killer. I admit I haven't had that pattern before."

"Me neither." Matthew pointed toward the coffee pot, smiling invitingly. Jason made a face, as if Matthew had broken the coffee maker and all the china. "What about the reporter, Callahan? Did he use his survival story in the media?"

"He wrote a very emotional first article for his paper and praised his saviors as if they were angels coming for him. However, he didn't mention their names, which is a first in his career." Agent Drexler chuckled. "TV crews were all over the story, and he appeared in quite a few shows. Yes, he has made a fortune out of his adventure. I heard, though, that his girlfriend broke up with him and told a paper how stupid Callahan had been. She was shaken after the kidnapping, though Boswell didn't hurt her—he only carried her through the woods. She didn't forgive Callahan for inviting her on this trip with the clear intention of investigating the killer's methods."

"Understandable."

"Boswell faces a life in prison, even though his victims

have not yet been found. For now he's being held for kidnapping and attempted murder. Police and other services are searching the area with dogs, but it looks like he drove his victims far away. The elderly couple we interrogated after Agent Hayes's description denies any knowledge of their nephew being a killer. They claim he is an upstanding citizen who helps people." Drexler snorted. "I bet they would say anything in his favor. What about Callahan's saviors—Agent Hayes and his fiancé? Are they all right? Did they return safely?"

"Her parents looked after them," Jason said as he returned with a cup of coffee. "He told me yesterday that he didn't wish for anything more than to return home and go to bed. If you ask me, I guess they'll be still asleep." He rolled his eyes when Matthew chuckled.

"You've got a brave fellow agent. Do you know how they escaped Boswell's trap?"

"I have no idea. We talked on the phone, but I don't expect his report for a day or two."

"Please, send me a copy. I saw the hole in the ground, and it was deep—frighteningly deep. I wouldn't want to be locked up in there."

Matthew saw Jason shudder. "We're all happy it turned out the way it did. Callahan has his big story, and our fellow agent some more free days for recovery."

Jacklyn was tempted to film their session. It was a rare occasion that Nicolas allowed her to play with him throughout the day and use a variety of toys. Though she wasn't surprised he needed to shed responsibility, she hid her surprise when he asked her to extend their game from the bedroom to the entire house, and that he didn't wish to go without shackles. He escaped into a scenario Jacklyn described as *No Decision Day*. It wasn't unheard of that men who shouldered great responsibility needed time to push away all decisions and be happy with being ordered around.

The first peak of arousal in the morning was over, and since Nicolas had come early and without permission, she had used the moment to scold him and changed his tethers. He knelt beside her, blindfolded, collared, and handcuffed while she fed him bits from the breakfast table. He looked lovely in chains and leather.

Unable to hold back, she excused herself and fetched a camera while he didn't notice. She grew wet between her legs seeing Nicolas sitting on his haunches waiting for her return, waiting for the game to continue. He looked utterly relaxed, even happy in a way she hadn't seen him for a long time.

Even though their vacation had turned in to a horrifying chase, it had triggered this development and a new insight into her lover's character. She hadn't lied that she knew him well enough to read his expression and sense his mood, but the intensity of his longing to submit to her wishes was overwhelming.

She took the leash that was attached to the collar and led him back to the bedroom, camera in the other hand. He walked beside her on hands and knees as if it was the most natural way to spend a free day. Jacklyn captured his moves on film, hardly able to restrain herself. She wanted to record every inch of his perfect body, so she ordered him to climb the spanking bench.

Nicolas moaned when she locked his wrists and ankles.

"No moaning, beast, or this will cost you."

Nicolas moaned all the louder, and Jacklyn laughed as she put the camera on a nightstand so she could tape the session.

Maybe she would show him the video one day. Maybe she would use it to lift her mood when she was sad or angry.

Aroused from head to toe, Jacklyn reached for her many-

tailed whip. "I told you it will cost you. Here you go."
 Nicolas exhaled. "My wonderful Belle . . . ouch!"

CHAPTER EIGHTEEN

Jason was the happiest man in DC. His best friend and partner was back on the job after a ten-day trip to Miami. When he picked up the phone, he was almost singing his own name to the caller.

"This is Harold Foster. Do you remember me?"

Jason's mood dropped a notch. "Of course, I remember you. How are you?"

"Much better, thank you."

"And Mr. Winters?"

"In fact, he's the reason I'm calling you. After five long days in which I did not know if he would survive, he's now responsive again. Not out of the woods yet, but he'll mend. He's asking for you."

Jason inhaled and wiped the bridge of his nose, pondering.

"I know that I'm asking a lot of you," Foster said when the pause continued. "But it would mean a lot to him."

Jason tried to prepare himself for the conversation, to come up with a few non-binding sentences that he could say and then apologize as quickly as possible and leave again. He stood at the door to the hospital room, and his mind was blank. Harold Foster sat on a chair, his reading glasses on his nose, reading to Terry from the local newspaper. Terry Winters lay propped on a thick pillow and listened. He was pale and haggard, his hair grown out. He was still being fed intravenously, and the heart monitor close to the bed was switched on.

Jason lowered his chin, exhaled, and then opened the door, heart beating in his throat.

Harold took off his glasses, got up, and came to shake hands. "Hello, Agent Beckham, it's good to see you."

Jason nodded.

Behind them, Terry's face lit up with happiness. "Agent Beckham, I'm so glad to see you. How come you are here?"

Without Terry noticing, Harold smiled, and Jason understood that Harold hadn't told him about their conversation.

"I was in the area," Jason stammered as he walked toward the foot of the bed. "How are you doing?"

Terry's happiness and smile were genuine, contagious. "I'm alive because of you. I'm so happy I can thank you in person for what you did for me."

Jason was tempted to say that he had just done his job, but Terry's soft features, stressed from the ordeal he had survived, forbade such harsh, rejecting words. "It wasn't me alone. The medic was great, and the ambulance came quickly. The doctors here are the real heroes."

"I know that you prayed for me," Terry said and lifted his right hand. "You held my hand, told me that I must hang on so that I would see Harold again. You told me not to let go."

Jason felt a shiver down his spine. For his life, he hadn't expected that Terry had been aware of his words.

"You were there when I needed hope. You kept your word and didn't let me die."

Jason vividly remembered his blood-covered hands after Terry had been taken away and how he had felt, not knowing whether the young man would survive. He bridged the distance and took Terry's hand in his, moved in a way he hadn't thought possible. "I'm more than happy that you are alive," he said quietly. "We had made every effort to find you in time."

"You did." Terry squeezed Jason's hand. "Thank you.

Thank you so much."

When Jason couldn't find any words, Harold stepped in. "Thank you for stopping by, Agent Beckham."

"Jason."

"Very well."

Harold smiled at him, and the open gratitude of both men was too much to bear. Jason apologized, said that he had to leave and went back to the corridor.

Harold followed him and asked quietly, "Is it so hard to handle gratitude?" He cocked his head, and a small understanding smile played around his lips. "We are all confronted with criticism and the harshness of business. We've forgotten that there's goodness and gratitude. It's the utmost gift to be there in a moment of dire need. You should know, Terry regained consciousness five days ago, and when he could talk again, he asked me to contact you. He repeated that he wouldn't have made it without you. Yes, you can claim that you are no doctor, but your presence was vital. And you can't tell me that those were empty words."

Jason shook his head, all of his eloquence gone.

"Come back, visit him again. I know he will be happy to see you. So would I."

Jason looked into Harold's benevolent eyes and nodded. "I'll do that." He wasn't astonished at the words themselves but that he truly meant what he said.

Harold patted his shoulder as he turned to leave. "I'll see you around, then."

Jason left the hospital and called Elaine to tell her that he loved her.

The End

ABOUT THE AUTHOR

Ann Raina lives and works in Germany with cats and a horse. Riding and writing are her favorite hobbies. So far, she has written twenty-six novels for eXtasy Books with more to come. Her latest series, starting with *Twisted Mind*, deals with FBI Agent Nicolas Hayes, his cases of capital crimes, and his demanding and commanding lover, Jacklyn Hollander.

In all of her books she combines romance, suspense, and humorous elements, for no thrilling story can stand without a comic relief.

For contact turn to annraina@yahoo.com

On Facebook https://www.facebook.com/ann.raina.7

On Instagram: ann_raina_author

www.ingramcontent.com/pod-product-compliance
Lightning Source LLC
Chambersburg PA
CBHW070824120626
46556CB00002B/653